MW01488749

1

A young man stood on his porch, trying to throw a rope up and over a beam. He was shirtless and in boxers. Mort was presented the sight of his musculature working in the sweaty evening, a gleaming sheen that highlighted the sinewy lines of his body. There was something very innocent about the sight, even as his face contorted with frustration when the end of the rope flopped back down on the wrong side of the rafter. A soft sob made its way to Mort, the only wet thing in an ocean of dry.

The man did not notice he was being watched. They never did. They were always so preoccupied with bringing an end to things. They thought they were alone. But he was always there. It was one of the many sorrows of his business, watching the lie of isolation claim lives.

"Are you really quitting?"

Mort looked over his shoulder. His cousin was standing behind him. Kitten hissed at the dog-headed Anubis and took refuge in Mort's hood. Mort glanced at Anubis briefly, then turned his attention back to the suicide.

"Yes."

"So why are you here?" Anubis always spoke in a soft growl.

"Coincidence."

His cousin smiled, sharp canines flashing in desert sun. "We both know better than to believe in coincidences. You are here because you are meant to be here."

"You can go," Mort said. "I have this in hand."

"But you are no longer conducting souls. You are no longer a psychopomp. What good can you do him?"

"You can go," Mort repeated, his teeth gritted, the hollow of his eye flashing dark for a moment in a revelation of his true self. "I have this in hand."

"How? Oh. *Ohhhhh....*" The last oh was drawn out in a kind of mocking pity. "Oh, you're not going to try to save him, are you? How perfectly pathetic."

The man had succeeded in finally getting the end of his rope over the rafter, an achievement that bought him no joy whatsoever. He tugged on the rope, finding it suitably sturdy. He then began to construct the wrong kind of knot.

Mort stood in the driveway and watched while the kitten in his hood purred. He observed the man closely, his gaze taking in the way his dirty blond hair fell just shy of his shoulders. Sweat was beading in the bristle along his jawline. He hadn't shaved. His physique was powerful, but not bulky. He had the frame of a survivor, in spite of the fact he was very much engaged in attempting the opposite.

He had no sense of his beauty or uniqueness. He did not see himself the way Mort did. His expression was contorted in the kind of self-reproach and loathing that showed he was actively hating himself even while trying to end himself. There was no compassion, no forgiveness, only a fixated, narrow view of what he imagined would be the end.

He was beauty trapped in human form, completely unappreciative of itself, and entirely incapable of such appreciation. Misery hung about him in a cloud so thick that to Mort's eyes it seemed to fuzz the scene ever so slightly.

Mort ignored Anubis, stepped forward and into the fray of human suffering, putting one heavy booted foot on the lowest step. The wood creaked.

The man looking for his end turned around and stared at him.

"What do you want?"

The question was abrupt and rude, and it did not bother Mort one bit.

"Don't," Mort said.

They exchanged looks, and in those looks much was silently said. Mort felt the depth of the man's despair and could offer little comfort. The man, for his part, suddenly felt the eternity of cold that stood behind Mort, the endless nothing. Many people flee from that sensation. He did not.

"Why not? Because life is worth living?"

"It won't work."

The man looked back at the rope again.

It was a little frustrating not knowing the man's name. If Mort had been working, he would have had the book with all the names. Now he had nothing. He did not know if the man was a sinner or a saint, if he was heaven or hell bound. He did not even know if it was the man's time.

This must be what it was to be human, to know absolutely nothing whatsoever and yet be forced to go about the place as if it all made sense.

He stepped up onto the porch and took the rope from the man's hands. "Go inside," he said. "Drink some lemonade."

He had a feeling there would be lemonade inside in a pitcher the man's mother used to own. It would be sweet and flat, and it would anchor him to life once more.

The man stared at him for a long moment, and then nodded mutely. He was content to be told what to do because he had not planned to be doing anything.

"Wait." Mort said, hardly believing this was the first time he had ever had to ask this particular question. "What is your name?"

The man paused at the weather worn door of his home and looked back at Mort with a pale, sad gaze.

"Tristan."

Perfect.

T*ristan*

A stranger stood on Mama's old porch and told him he couldn't die today. If he didn't know better, he would have called it divine intervention.

Mama's lemonade sat in the fridge, as it always had. Tristan hadn't drunk it because he knew there would never be any more, and he was trying to save it. But the power had been cut off six weeks ago, and now it had a scum of green across the top. He hadn't been able to bring himself to throw it out.

Tristan stood in the kitchen with the fridge door open until he heard the front door creak open. The stranger was inside his house now, dark eyes boring into the back of his head.

"I'm Mort," the stranger said. "That's my name."

Though Mort was not a large guy, he was imposing. He felt like a big, heavy presence behind Tristan. An intrusion in his space. Tristan didn't let people come into his house, not since Mama passed. The house was filthy and embarrassing.

"Hi," Tristan said, as if they hadn't already met outside on the porch. "I don't think I should drink this."

Mort looked over his shoulder at Mama's lemonade. Tristan felt him as a long, looming creature, even though he didn't seem to be that inordinately tall. No more than six foot one at the very most, and Tristan himself was over six feet. So.

"Perhaps not," Mort agreed.

Tristan turned to him, his slow brain finally starting to work on the normal questions of human interaction. "Are you here from the power company? A bailiff? Do you have some kind of summons for me? I have to tell you, bud. I'm not planning on making any appearances anywhere anytime soon."

He plucked a warm beer from the six pack on the counter. There was one left in its wake. The rings of several other six packs were stacked on the counter. He made sure to cut them up so they didn't kill penguins. Weren't many penguins in the desert, but these things traveled. Shipped out of state, and out of the country half the time, around the globe to a third world nation where it had an even chance of being poured straight into a river.

"I suppose I could be bailiff of sorts," Mort said. "But I am not on duty. Actually, I quit."

Tristan felt an immediate kinship. "Yeah? Good for you, buddy. I got fired from my last job."

"Oh?"

"Yep."

The awkwardness drew out between them.

"So," Tristan said, taking a sip of his beer. "Why are you here?"

"I don't know," Mort said, bluntly and boldly, as if that lack of knowledge did not bother him one bit. Almost as if he was proud of it. So he was a drifter, then. A hobo who simply happened to have wandered up to Tristan's house at the same time as... it felt embarrassing to think about what he'd been caught doing. It already felt like a weird faux pas more than a crisis.

"Do you want a beer?" Tristan made the offer to break the awkwardness.

"Yes. Thank you."

Tristan handed his guest the other beer, and together they drank in silence. The beer wasn't helping to clear his head, but it was calming him down. He was already somewhat glad he'd been interrupted out on the porch. The urge to no longer exist was starting to retreat. The pain was waning into the alcohol. Maybe things were going to be okay. Ha.

Mort didn't say anything. Mort drank the beer in one long, continuous swallowing motion, like it was water.

As the urgency of ending himself subsided, Tristan inspected his guest. When he looked at Mort in certain lights, his face seemed gaunt. Maybe gaunt wasn't the right word. More like skeletal. Tristan felt as though he was seeing flashes through the skin, something like bone. Obviously, that couldn't be true. His mind was playing tricks on him again. It had been playing tricks for a while. Showing him things that weren't there.

Drinking usually helped to not see things. It dulled his senses and made him feel warm, fuzzy, and comfortable. Maybe he needed another beer.

He reached for the last beer, forgetting he'd given it to the stranger.

Shit. He was out. He felt an immediate surge of anxiety. He couldn't be out. Life without beer, well, it wasn't worth living.

"Need more beer," Tristan said. "Gotta go to the store. Guess I'll see you around."

Mort did not pick up on that cue.

"I will come with you."

"You got any money?" It was an audacious question, but Tristan had literally nothing to lose. If this hobo was going to hang around, he may as well chip in.

Mort reached into his pocket and pulled out a fat roll of twenties. There had to be thousands of dollars there. Tristan's eyes widened.

"Alright," he said. "You're buying."

"Very well," Mort agreed.

This was getting stranger and stranger by the moment, but Tristan wasn't going to question free beer.

He went back and put some jeans and boots on. He didn't bother with a shirt. This was all too good to be true. And probably a figment of his imagination. Not once in Tristan's twenty-seven years had he ever been saved by anyone. Why would that start today? He thoroughly expected to stumble back into the kitchen and discover the screen door banging against the siding of the house, nobody to be seen for miles.

To his surprise, Mort was waiting when he came back. He looked very real and very solid, standing in the kitchen, his hands in the pockets of his jeans. Something furry was twitching by his neck, and another pair of eyes was observing Tristan.

Mort had a kitten in his hood, Tristan noticed for the first time. The little black thing was curled up around the back of his neck very comfortably. That would have given most people a cozy appearance, but with Mort it only served to highlight his gaunt, elegant energy. Mort's boots were red with dust, his jeans looked marked and ripped. He had all the signs of having been on foot for a long time, but there was none of the desperation or madness that accompanied true strays. He wasn't displaced from the world. If Tristan had to say, he would have guessed Mort was entirely separate from it.

"Ready to go?" The question slipped comfortably out between Mort's lips as if it had been asked thousands of times before.

"Uh. Sure."

Tristan tried to cover for his surprise. He had truly expected to find Mort gone. There was nothing to stay for here, not in this filthy old house rotting from the inside out. Even he didn't want to be here anymore. But Mort was here. Waiting.

What kind of a person interrupted a guy killing himself and bought him beer?

A good person, that's who. In Tristan's experience, there were no such things as good people, so this was turning out to be a very strange day all around.

They passed the noose on the way out. Tristan hooked a finger in it to make it swing. It didn't occur to him how ghoulish it would look until he spotted the reflection in the house window.

Oh well.

Mort didn't seem bothered by it. Mort didn't seem bothered by much. He had a slightly melancholy but otherwise calm air. Most people got very weird around death, but Mort barely seemed to notice it. He hadn't mentioned it. Maybe he was trying to be polite. That was something good people were rumored to do from time to time.

"Truck's broken down, we'll have to walk," Tristan said as they passed the old, rusted-out piece of junk that hadn't run in years.

"I like being on foot," Mort said as they set out together. "I also enjoy riding."

"Horses?"

"I have a horse at home," Mort said.

"And where's that?"

"Hell."

Tristan laughed, a good belly laugh that drew fresh desert air into his lungs and chased away the stench of misery that had been lurking in there.

Mort smiled ever so slightly, making Tristan think he appreciated his own joke.

"I'm from Hell too," Tristan said, feeling much better.

He was, of course, curious about his visitor. As they walked down the dusty road, he started to ask questions.

"So you're not from around here, and you walked here, and you have a cat."

"I have a cat?" Mort seemed surprised by that revelation.

Tristan pointed to the kitten in his hood.

"Oh," Mort said. "That cat."

For the first time in what felt like a very long time, Tristan cracked a real smile. "You're the weirdest fucking guy I ever met. Normally I'm the weird one."

"I am much stranger than you," Mort agreed.

The walk to the store, generally an arduous slog he had to stumble through as best he could with only the promise of a cool beer to drive him, seemed to fly by. They seemed to be there in an instant.

The store wasn't really a store. It was a gas station where the only fresh, clean thing was the case of scratcher tickets that sold out frequently. The town was a big believer in luck, though nobody had ever won more than fifty bucks. It was commonly believed that they were collectively due a big win, as if the scratchers were a poker machine that hadn't paid out in a while.

"Two scratchers," Tristan said. "And two six packs, please."

Earl was behind the counter as usual. He was a husky guy in his sixties. He had a stained shirt with an alligator on it, an oxygen tank, and a smoking habit. Tobacco smoke curled yellow in front of the old no-smoking sign.

Neither one of them bothered with pleasantries. Mort paid the bill and carried one of the six packs back outside. Tristan usually drank out the back, and today was no different. He led Mort around the rear where upside down crates waited for them between piles of old tires and barrels of whatever.

He sat down, cracked a beer, and took a long draught. Mort sat beside him, saying nothing.

"So. Why are you in town?" Tristan asked the question when he had swallowed.

"I have nowhere else to be."

"I feel that," Tristan said. The cold beer was starting to make him feel better. It was weird. He hadn't planned on being here to see the sunny afternoon, but he was suddenly quite glad he was. Nothing had materially changed. He was still deeply miserable, but the moment of intense crisis had passed, and there was a distraction from the morass of his own internal state.

In the bright light of a desert afternoon, Tristan inspected the face of his new friend. Mort had quite thick dark hair, and the kind of face that was difficult to place in terms of age. He could have been twenty, or perhaps forty. At some angles, he seemed young, but when his dark gaze met Tristan's, there was an agelessness to it. Actually, there was a complete lessness to it — *lessness* not being a word until that very moment, when Tristan felt the void he had always felt inside him somehow now regarding him from the outside. It was a more comforting sensation than one might expect. All his life, he had felt a certain distance and difference from the people around him, like he was living in a world not quite the same as them. He did not feel that with this guy. He felt a kinship.

"If you're looking to crash somewhere for a while, I have a spare room," he offered. "You're welcome to use it."

"Very generous," Mort intoned. He did have a very resonant, deep voice. He sounded like someone much larger. It was hard to tell what kind of build he really had. The hoodie he wore was oversized. He could be muscular underneath it, or he could be a skinny little guy.

"Alright. What do you want to eat? I'm hungry. The station has chimichangas. They're not bad. They're not good, either. But I haven't cooked or shopped in weeks. So."

Mort fisted a handful of bills from his roll and handed them over. There had to be at least a couple hundred bucks in Tristan's hand now.

"What do you want for all this? Are you going to ask me to suck your dick later or something?"

Mort looked back at him with dark eyes, giving nothing away. "That does not seem appropriate, given the circumstances."

"Then what do you want for this?"

"You said I could stay with you, did you not? I am compensating you for some of your hospitality."

M *ort*

Mort watched as Tristan disappeared back around the corner to get them some food. It was so easy to make a human happy. Money for food, money for beer, that's all Tristan needed for now.

The comment about dick sucking had not slid off him as easily as he had pretended it did. There had been a moment of frisson, a point at which he could have invited such attentions. But he had no intention of buying them.

As soon as Mort was completely alone, he heard a dark whisper on the wind.

"Interfering is against the rules. Quitting is one thing, but you know this is going to bring enforcement down on you. Your job is to conduct souls, not save them. Get up and leave now, before you get the pair of you into deep trouble."

"Leave me alone, Anubis," Mort hissed back. "I know what I am doing."

He heard Anubis chuckle, fainter now.

"You never know what you are doing."

2

Tristan stepped back through the front door of his home, walking past the rope still hanging with a half-noose in it from the porch rafter. He was chewing on his second chimichanga, and feeling something like normal, which for him was extraordinary.

It had been too long since he went for a walk with someone and just talked. Mort didn't say a lot, but he was a very good listener. Tristan had told him everything, about how he fucked up his life, and how his mama had gotten sick and left him the house, and how now he didn't have enough money to pay for it because he kept being fired from jobs, and there weren't that many jobs in Solitude anyway.

"So anyway, they said if they ever saw me again, they'd..."

He stopped talking abruptly.

There was a demon at the kitchen table.

A red creature slowly dripped something like sulphur and lava onto the floorboards, but somehow didn't catch them alight. It locked eyes with him and leered, a sharp, fanged smile. Sometimes Tristan mistook people for demons, but this wasn't human. It was too angular and too hungry. It smelled like rotten eggs, instantly putting him off his food.

Some basic instinct made him thrust the remnants of his chimichanga toward the creature. Better his snack be eaten than his soul. The demon leered, ignoring his offering. Deep red eyes seemed to fill the entirety of his vision, and suddenly he was falling into a pit of eternal despair. He felt the pointlessness return. He felt his worthlessness. He felt the noose swinging behind him. Suddenly, it was as though the walk had never happened, nor the conversation with a stranger fast becoming a friend. He was thrust back into the darkness of his life and his heart, and reminded that he was nothing to anyone, least of all to himself.

"DAMNED DEMON!"

Mort boomed the words, pushing past Tristan and putting himself between them. He was taller now, at least seven foot tall, or maybe Tristan was shrinking. Either option seemed to be a potential possibility.

The kitten in Mort's hood woke up and put two paws on his shoulder, arching its back and hissing with tiny feline fury. It was small and it was helpless, but it knew neither of those things about itself. Tristan found himself admiring the little thing. It was brave. He had never been brave. He definitely wasn't brave now. He would have run, but he was drunk and frozen in place. So he stood there and watched and listened.

"What are you doing here?" Mort made the demand with cool authority. He spoke to the demon like a middle-manager chastising a floor worker. It was not the only authoritarian interaction Tristan been party to, and the last time he experienced such a thing, he was the floor worker. It didn't end well for him. He did not think it would end well for this demon either.

"I am here to claim the soul." The demon spoke in a high pitch. If Tristan had met a person who sounded like that, he would never have been afraid of them. On a demon, it was terrifying.

"He's using his soul. He's alive." Mort's plain statement of fact came with a side of scathing, unspoken *idiot*.

"He relinquished it hours ago. A place was made."

"Then unmake it," Mort said simply. "Stack a different soul in his place. He is alive. Clearly. You've made a mistake."

"You know these places are not interchangeable." The demon shifted uncomfortably. It was not used to human furniture and it seemed unsure how to use it. "You should have brought him."

"I quit," Mort said.

"Then let me take him."

"No."

"You cannot save the damned."

"He doesn't need saving," Mort uttered through clenched teeth. "And he is not damned. He's not even fucking dead."

The demon shifted to perch on the chair, knees high, hands between its feet like a gargoyle. That seemed to make it more comfortable. "If you don't let me take him, the boss will come."

"Let him come," Mort said. "Now get the hell out of the house. BEGONE!"

At that final command, the demon disappeared in a flash of sulphur and flame, banished by the will of Mort.

"The fuck..." Tristan let out his breath.

The kitten shook its upright fluffy tail and settled back down, curling into Mort's hood, almost as if taking credit for the success of the interlude.

Mort turned to Tristan with an apologetic expression. "I am sorry. That must have seemed strange to you."

"I mean..."

"I do not yell at empty chairs often."

Tristan frowned. "The chair wasn't empty. It had a fuckin' demon in it."

Mort's dark brows rose. "You could see him?"

"Him? I'm not bold enough to assume that thing's gender. Whatever it was, they were clear as fucking day. I need another beer."

Mort looked at him with pale intensity, speaking as if the answer to the question really mattered very much. "What did you see. Tell me exactly."

"Red dude, sharp teeth, fiery eyes, claw hands..."

"Alright. Yes. That was the demon."

"Yeeeah," Tristan drew out the word with a sense of punctuating the obvious, as if Mort had just confirmed that yes, the sky was blue. "I figured."

"Interesting," Mort mused. "You should not be able to see demons."

Tristan cracked another beer. "Buddy, I've been surrounded by demons my whole fucking life."

3

Tristan had drunk himself into a stupor and fallen asleep in a bed in which the sheets had not been changed in months. He was still dressed in jeans and dusty boots, which either made it worse, or better. Mort could not tell.

Mort sat beside Tristan, watching him sleep. He felt deeply curious about this man who possessed greater gifts and potential than was indicated by his trappings, comportment, or surroundings. From time to time, humans were born with more talents than were useful to them. Those talents became burdens, and those burdens sometimes became anchors, dragging them down, out of the realm of the living. Some of these gifted people had a greater sense of the here-after plains, but he had never met one who could truly see demons.

The kitten emerged from his hood and walked down his arm, sniffing at Tristan. It had eaten the remnants of Mort's chimichanga and seemed satisfied now to curl up in the warmth of the man.

"You are miserable," he said to the sleeping man. "But..." He extended his fingers, rendered skeletal by the moonlight coming through the filthy window, brushing them through Tristan's rough, shorn locks. "You are also a mystery."

Mort had not come expecting to become invested in any particular human. He was actually very bored of people, really, but they were everywhere. Mort's very existence had been forged in service to these creatures. He was made for their ends.

If he had been working today, he would have waited for Tristan to finish what he was doing, and then he would have conducted the weeping shade to the hereafter. It would not have been his problem. It would have been his duty.

Instead, he sat and watched the young man snore, realizing he was going to have to put together information about him piece by piece.

There were family photos on the wall, and spaces where some of the photos seemed to have been moved after a long period of residence. Lighter wallpaper in squares and ovals. The ones that remained were pictures of an even younger Tristan, and his mother.

The woman was not a complete stranger. He recognized her face. He had conducted her somewhat recently, though not from this house. From a hospital in the nearest city, where she had been waiting for him, frail but ready. He did not think Tristan had not been there, but Mort would not have noticed him if he had been. When working, his focus was always entirely on his charge. The living were a vague blur of noise and movement.

He looked around the room. This seemed to be Tristan's childhood room. There were little trappings of an immature past still present, a model car atop a cupboard, and a yellow-edged certificate for a spelling bee that took place in the late nineties. The closet was open, and a letterman's jacket hung inside it. It didn't look like it had belonged to Tristan. It didn't look like it had been worn much at all.

Tristan himself was twenty-seven years old, he discovered when he found a half-completed college application from nine years ago. The papers were stuck inside a car magazine where they had been shoved and forgotten. He'd never gone, Mort gathered.

This was the room of a person who had stopped growing at eighteen and just gotten older. An adulthood existed but had never been claimed.

Mort shuffled further through the papers he found on what used to be Tristan's homework desk. He found pictures, scribbles, really.

There was a note on one, written in the tense hand of a teacher.

"Unrealistic."

Ironically, it was a near perfect sketch of a hellvore hound. But of course the teacher had never seen one, so she thought it nothing more than a poor rendering of a dog.

Mort looked around the room and saw squandered potential everywhere. Next to the bed, a pile of half-crushed beer cans demonstrated the numbing force of alcohol.

"You're special," Mort said. "And you're beautiful. And you are alive."

He spoke these truths to the insensate young man, who had begun snoring. The kitten started to purr, as if not wanting to be left out.

Satisfied that all were settled for the moment, Mort walked the entire house, peeked in every drawer, rifled through every family photo album. There was no indication anywhere of a father, but Mort knew how people were made and so surely there had to have been one, even if only for a few minutes.

Tristan awoke to his house more trashed than it usually was. It was as if a tornado had ripped through the trailer, throwing open every drawer and every cupboard and removing the contents. He found Mort in the kitchen, on hands and knees, looking under a chair.

"What the fuck did you do?"

Mort banged his head slightly as he got out from under the chair and stood up. He didn't rub the spot he hit. He didn't seem to register the pain at all.

The kitten was on the counter, licking something. Tristan didn't want to even begin to guess what.

"What are you doing?" It was worth asking the question again. Every single item in the kitchen, like every item in the trailer, had been taken out and put on chaotic display.

"I am getting to know you," Mort said.

"Dude. What the fuck is wrong with you?" Tristan's head hurt. He was not a clean and tidy person, but just because he was okay with his own mess didn't mean Mort was welcome to add to it.

"I don't know," Mort said with that charming simplicity. He wasn't being an asshole. He was just absent of appropriateness.

"If you're going to make a mess, clean it up."

"I'm sorry. Nothing in your home suggested you cared about tidiness."

Coming from anybody else that would have been a sassy read. But Mort didn't have any attitude. He was simply telling the truth as he saw it.

"Me making a mess is one thing. You making a mess is rude."

"Oh," Mort said. "Then I should clean up."

Tristan was going to tell him not to bother, but there was so much of a mess he couldn't even get to his morning breakfast beer.

"Why did you go through my family albums?" He asked the question as he attempted to pick his way through the loose piles of garbage and treasured family heirlooms.

"I was curious."

"About what?"

Mort looked at him simply. "About you."

"You can just ask me questions."

"You were asleep. Actually, you were unconscious from alcohol, and then you fell asleep."

Again, no judgement. Just bald statements of fact.

There was something insulting yet charming about Mort. Tristan knew he should probably be kicking this guy out of his house, but he didn't have the urge to actually do it.

"It's pretty rude and creepy to go through people's things."

"Is it? I suppose that makes sense."

Tristan leaned back against the countertop, upon which all the spoons in the house had been laid out with an odd specificity. Having reached the beer, his mood improved considerably. There was no sound like the sound of a tab being pulled in the morning. Or maybe afternoon. Hard to tell what time of day it really was. That sort of thing had stopped mattering quite a while ago.

"I was looking for clues as to why you see demons."

"I don't think you're going to find any clues here," Tristan said.

"Maybe not. Maybe I will find clues in what is not here."

Tristan drank half his beer while Mort began to tidy things up again, slowly but efficiently. He turned to Tristan with a plate that had been used a good month ago, if not longer.

"Where would you like your mold-covered pasta to go?"

"Throw it out, I guess."

Mort had never intended on tidying the house, but it seemed to be the natural progression of putting things back together.

"I'll do the dishes," Tristan said, giving voice to the phrase with a certain amount of self-surprise. "Haven't done them in about three months."

"I'll dry," Mort said. "I've always wanted to try that."

"God, you're fucking weird," Tristan laughed.

Mort wondered vaguely how he might appear more normal, but he was truly not too worried about it. Tristan appeared delighted by his oddities, and Mort was not worried about anybody else's opinion.

The house was still filthy when they were done, but one part of it was a different kind of dirty. The kitchen counters were clear and had been wiped down, and the dishes that had festooned every inch of space were now stacked tidily in what had been empty cupboards.

The refrigerator had also been emptied and cleaned out. The jug that had held the rancid lemonade now sat upside down on the draining board, sparkling clean, if somewhat sudsy.

"So," Tristan said. "Where are you headed?"

Mort misunderstood the intent of the question completely.

"I am here." Mort said. "I could be anywhere, but I am here. People do not put enough thought into the oddness of the state of their circumstances. Why here and not there? Why now and not then?"

"People do think about that, but there are never any fucking answers," Tristan said. "So they either pick an answer, accept that there is no answer they can know, or get very smug insisting that there's no answer because it's all random and nothing matters."

He took another swig of his breakfast beer, which, given the hour of the day, was beginning to become his lunch beer.

"There is no food here," Mort noticed. "We will need food."

"So you're staying?"

Mort fixed him with a determined glare. "I am staying until I understand why you can see demons."

"Could be a while."

"I have all the time in the universe." Mort sat down at the kitchen table, which had not been completely cleared of all debris. A pair of Tristan's boots sat in front of him, filthy with mud and oil. "Tell me about the first time you saw a demon."

Tristan didn't remember much about his early life, but he did remember that.

"I was seven years old. My mom had guests. One of them didn't look like a person to me. I tried to tell her, but I wasn't supposed to see the guests at all. She only invited them after I was asleep, and they never stayed longer than thirty minutes."

"Very orderly," Mort said, missing the point. He did that a lot. Whatever he'd been doing, and wherever he'd come from, it wasn't anywhere like around here.

"She was selling her ass," Tristan said bluntly. "To truckers, mostly. This place is right off the highway."

"Oh," Mort said. He didn't seem to be judging, but Tristan was.

"It wasn't so bad. It kept me fed, and put clothes on my back, and some of her regulars would drop off extra things to us. I got a football one year. But the older I got..." He stopped talking.

"Anyway," he said. "One of the guests when I was younger. He smelled like rotten eggs. I'd always know when he was here. One night, I crept out to see him, and he looked a lot like the guy I just saw. Red eyes, tail, hooves, horns. I screamed, and my mom came out to see what was wrong, and then..." He shut his eyes and shook his head, as if trying to dislodge the memory. "He told her not to worry, that I'd gotten a fright, and he took her back into her bedroom."

Mort stayed sitting, listening, still and focused. Tristan shifted uncomfortably, not used to being looked at like that.

"I tried telling her the next day, but she thought it was a lie. She thought I was making things up because I didn't like her 'friends'. I got in trouble for being up so late." Tristan took a long swig. "That's when I started drinking. If I sipped a little of the beer from her friends' cans, I slept. I didn't have to hear the... sounds."

Mort's expression was serious and very engaged. He was listening, truly listening.

"That is a very inappropriate experience for someone of that age."

"I had a lot of inappropriate experiences," Tristan said.

Mort nodded solemnly. "Terrible as they are, they do not explain why you were able to discern the nature of the visitor."

Tristan shrugged again. "Saw a shrink once who said it was probably a trauma response."

"If that were true, everyone would see demons."

"That's what I said."

"And what did they say?"

Tristan thought about it a second. "Well, a few things. But mostly they said, '*Ow, stop hitting me.*'"

Mort flickered a brow. "You hit a therapist? Why?"

"I had anger issues when I was a teenager. Something about random dudes coming to my house to fuck my mom. I used to hit a lot of people. Don't worry. I'm not going to hit you."

Mort laughed at that piece of reassurance. "Very kind of you."

Tristan's eyes narrowed slightly as he examined Mort with all the beer-soaked insight he could muster. "You're really not afraid of me, huh? Most people around here don't want anything to do with me. But you're not from around here. Where are you from?"

"Like I said," Mort replied. "Hell. Let's go shopping. This house needs food."

"Only way to get groceries, if that's what you mean, is to head out of Solitude and go to Perdition. It's about thirteen miles from here."

The entire region had been settled by depressed miners, which explained a lot in terms of place names.

"Let me guess. We're going to have to walk?"

"Yep."

"That's a long walk,"

"Yep. It's why my diet is beer and gas station food. Short drive, long walk."

"Then we will need a vehicle."

Mort did not need a vehicle, but Tristan was in no shape to walk twenty-six miles in a day.

"Truck died years ago," Tristan said.

"Let me take a look at it," Mort said.

"You a mechanic?"

"I'm used to broken things."

~

Tristan propped the hood of the truck up on a piece of two by four. The struts had long since rusted away. Mort looked into the motor, seeing several obvious issues immediately. The wiring had been gnawed away by rats, and there were remnants of a nest in the carburetor. He did not know the actual words for any of these things, but he knew that this much organic matter inside a machine was a bad thing.

"The garage we walked to. I mean, the gas station, there was a garage attached to it, no?"

"Yeah. Tom's garage."

"Alright, let's get Tom here and see what he can do."

"Eeergghhh..." Tristan made a less than encouraging sound. "Probably best he doesn't see me."

"Why not?"

"He's not a fan," Tristan explained.

Mort decided to leave that piece of interpersonal drama alone for the moment. Tristan's background was clearly fraught with conflict.

Mort walked to the garage alone, leaving Tristan behind at home. There he found an overall-clad figure he presumed to be the local mechanic.

"There's a truck that needs to be fixed. Owned by Tristan..." Mort realized he didn't know Tristan's last name, though he had definitely read it on the documents. Brown? He wanted to say Brown. No. Not Brown. It started with S.

The mechanic hadn't looked at him yet. He was too busy fiddling around with a bit of engine and too arrogant to care about a customer. People out here were not nearly so obsessed with pretending to give a shit about business. They did what they wanted, and most of the time they didn't want to do anything.

"Yeah, can't take that job, buddy. Sorry. Better buy yourself another piece of shit."

"Look at me, please." Mort spoke calmly but firmly.

Tom swung around, ready to mouth off. But the arrogant aggression faded the second he saw Mort's true face.

Mechanic Tom stared at him, slack jawed, in the way normal mortals responded to Mort's presence. It was a trance state of sorts. Tom wouldn't remember this conversation consciously, but it would still be somewhere inside him. Right now, Mort was speaking to the deeper, older parts of the mechanic. He'd bypassed all the social layers and was connecting with the real man.

Tom was about the same age as Tristan. Bulky, with the beginnings of a beer belly, brown hair and brown eyes. Handsome in the way Mort had always been indifferent to.

"Go to Tristan's house and mend it," Mort said, issuing the order in a calm but deep tone. "And lend me your vehicle. I wish to drive to the supermarket."

He could almost giggle at having had to form that sentence. It was just so pedestrian, so mortal. He was enjoying playing at being a person, having concerns and cares that obviously didn't matter at all and yet somehow seemed to matter more than anything.

Tom nodded in the way people tended to do when Mort asked them to do something. "Sure, I'll go around to the old whore's place, and..."

"That's a disrespectful manner of speaking about the home of a client," Mort corrected him smoothly.

"Uh. Sorry. It's just what everybody in town has always called that house."

"Then everybody in town is unkind."

"Yeah, we're a pack of assholes," Tom agreed without hesitation, still in trance. "She was the prettiest lady around, and we all knew it. But she'd fuck other women's husbands for money."

"Sounds to me as though she saved them a burden."

"They hated her. The women, and the husbands too. Nobody loves a whore. And nobody respects the son of a whore."

"You will respect Tristan. You will treat him like a person. You will fix his vehicle, and you will help him if he needs help in the future. You will do these things because he is not the son of a whore. He is a man of strength and worth, due equal if not greater respect than the others of you, because his life has been harder. Understand?"

"Yes, sir," Tom said. "I understand."

"Good. Then go."

"What...the..."

Mort turned to see Tristan behind him. He'd put an old t-shirt on and heavy boots. Ass-kicking boots. He looked worried. And adorable.

"Hey, Tristan," Tom said as he walked past. "I'm going to take a look at that truck of yours."

"Thanks?" Tristan seemed uncertain as to how to reply.

Tom stopped and fished his keys out of his pocket. "Take my car as a loaner until I get yours going."

"Uh..."

Tom was out, walking toward Tristan's home. Tristan looked at Mort with surprised blue eyes.

"You came after me," Mort noted. He also noted that he had none of his normal sway over Tristan. Tristan didn't go blank and willing. He didn't become an empty vessel for Mort's commands. Instead, he stayed steadfastly himself, perhaps one of the most alive people Mort had ever met.

Tristan scratched his head. "Well, yeah. I was worried Tom would kick your ass. I didn't think you'd be here talking me up to the school bully." He looked at Mort with wonder. "I've never had anybody stand up for me before."

"Get used to it," Mort said. The response came easily and automatically.

Tristan went an uncomfortable shade of pink and broke eye contact. "Guess we should get some of that food you wanted."

"Good idea."

4

nother night, another dark visitor. Mort felt the disturbance while Tristan slept, and was determined not to allow this guest to disturb his boy.

Mort was prepared to dismiss another demon, but the visage that appeared on the porch was not of a generic entity spawned from the bowels of Hell. It was a familiar face, one he had long known. All the attitude drained from his face in an instant, all the dominance gone as a shining creature stepped through a portal of its own making, accompanied by the unmistakeable volcanic scent of myrrh.

He was tall and broad, and he wore armor. He carried a spear too, strapped to his back. It would not be crazy for someone to be afraid of him, but Mort knew he had nothing to fear from this particular damned warrior.

"Balthazar." Mort greeted him on the front porch.

"There you are!" Balthazar said. "I have been worried about you."

Balthazar was a king and a lifelong friend to Mort, in the way one's father's friends can be one's own friends as one grows to maturity.

Balthazar had a well-trimmed beard and the type of face one sees depicted on ancient reliefs and relics. His eyes were deep and wide and expressive, his nose slightly hooked. His features were strong, as was his jaw and cheek-bones. He was handsome beyond handsome and absolutely regal.

Mort had a sudden rush of homesickness looking at him. It took all his energy not to regress and throw himself into the warrior king's arms for a hug.

"Don't worry about me," Mort said, trying to stop his lower lip from quivering at the emotion of seeing Balthazar here on the mortal plane. He knew how B hated this place.

"Anubis said you quit." Balthazar said the words in a tone of gentle concern.

"I did."

"Why?"

"I don't want to explain right now."

"Is it because of him?" Balthazar gestured a flaming arm to the sleeping Tristan, visible through the window. "You wouldn't be the first of us to develop a fascination with a mortal, but you cannot follow that urge. It destroys them. It robs them of what little life and choice is truly theirs. You know this."

"I'm not robbing him of anything," Mort argued, but even as he did, guilt was sinking through him. A deep, primal, elemental kind of guilt, the sort of feeling that came from the very origin of feelings.

"You have a purpose, Mort. If you deny that purpose, only misfortune will follow." Balthazar reached out, ruffling Mort's already messy hair. He had not brushed it since he quit. "You know I've got a soft spot for you, kid. I don't want to see you hurt."

"I'm not going to get hurt."

"The longer you spend up here, the thinner your connection to the astral planes becomes," B reminded him. "You're always going to be of our world, but you risk forgetting that, and once you forget, you can find yourself trapped here, going through the same things they go through. Living the amnesia of the mortal."

"I'm not going to stay that long."

Balthazar nodded. "It is your eternity to do with as you please. But I must warn you. Eventually, your father will come. And when he does, he will not be kind. Do not be caught with a mortal you care about. Remember, he is a torturer."

"I have not seen my father in over a thousand years," Mort replied. "I doubt he's going to show up any time soon. I'm far from his only son."

Balthazar's expression shifted slightly to something with a shade of pity.

"You've served well and long," he said. "You deserve a vacation. Just. Please, Mort. Do not get attached."

The kitten in Mort's hood was purring and kneading the back of Mort's neck, tiny little claws sinking into the first layers of his skin and pulling back to make tiny scratches.

"I won't," Mort promised.

"Then I will leave you be."

"Wait." Mort reached out before B left. "What can you tell me about this guy?"

Balthazar looked at the sleeping Tristan. "He's just a man."

"He's not just a man. He can see demons. And he's not afraid of me. And he doesn't fall into a trance when I'm near."

"Oh," Balthazar said. "Then he is a broken man."

"What?"

"An intact man cannot see these things because the shielding around him is intact. He is kept in the mortal plane in a protective sac, as it were. If that sac is broken somehow, parts of the astral can begin to leak. In those cases, a mortal might begin to perceive things outside his normal ability."

The explanation was simpler, sadder, and less dramatic than Mort had hoped.

"I thought perhaps he was special. Maybe he had some astral blood."

"Mortals break one another in thousands of ways," B said. "And some of them particularly love to destroy their children before their children have any chance to discover what they might have been, or who they could have become without pain. Like trees growing in a hostile wind, these people twist and grow into strange forms, sideways instead of up, or even around in spirals. Sometimes they are beautiful, but it is not because they are a different kind of tree. It is because of what shaped them."

Balthazar was wise, but wisdom did not always bring joy.

"I must leave now, before I am missed. We cannot have your father searching for two runaways, can we?" Balthazar smiled kindly. "Make good choices, Mort."

With that, he was gone.

The kitten stopped kneading, but it remained purring.

"I know," Mort said. "I like him too."

5

Tristan woke up thirsty. He stumbled out of bed and moved through the house in the slightly unco-ordinated way he always did before and, to be fair, after he drank.

It was morning. He wasn't used to mornings. Usually, he rose sometime around one, or maybe three in the afternoon. The morning was very bright, obnoxiously cheerful.

He found Mort in the kitchen.

"Where's the beer?"

"Why don't you have..." Mort checked the box with the brightly colored bird on it. "Cereal."

Tristan felt a spike of anxiety. "Where's the fucking beer?"

"In the refrigerator," Mort replied, deadpan.

"Oh. Right. Thanks." Tristan bent down and went into the refrigerator, where two six packs of beer made twelve blessed cans.

"You become rude over beer," Mort observed. "You treat a friend like an enemy."

"I guess. Sorry. Mama used to hide the beer, or worse, pour it out. She said I drank too much."

"You do drink too much."

"I know. But that's not anybody else's problem."

Mort cocked his head to the side slightly. "Do you believe that when you say it? Or does the lie curdle on your tongue even as you speak it?"

Tristan swallowed, already feeling better. He was used to defending his drinking. He defended it every day to himself. He'd tell himself that it wasn't that bad, because it was only beer. Real alcoholics drank whiskey. And who cared if he was an alcoholic? Plenty of people were.

He didn't reply to Mort, because he already knew those excuses, flimsy as they were, would not fly with Mort. He would dismiss them instantly and then they would be useless to himself as well.

"I don't ever see you eat," Tristan said.

Mort gave a slight shrug. In morning light, the very tips of his dark hair seemed slightly blond. Or maybe red. "I don't eat much."

"Don't each much, or can't eat at all?"

The mutual insight rendered them both silent, neither one of them wanting to admit their perceived shortcomings.

Tristan drank his beer. Mort ate nothing. The cereal went untouched.

Now that Mort knew the reason for Tristan's gift, or at least the reason Balthazar had given him, he wondered if the mystery might evaporate, and along with it, his interest.

Just a broken boy, hurt so deeply he saw demons.

The explanation was so reductive. It made something exciting and mysterious banal and sad.

He could leave now. Should leave now.

But the noose still hung on the porch, and he knew what would likely become of Tristan if he was to leave now. Nothing had changed. Nothing had been fixed.

"You thinking about moving on?" Tristan asked him the question, showing surprising perceptiveness for a drunk. "I've seen that expression before. People always leave."

"I don't want to leave," Mort said, surprised that it was true.

"You like shitty, broken-down houses, and assholes who day-drink? You said you were going to stay until you found out how I could see demons. Does this mean you've figured me out?"

"I think there is a simple and reductive explanation, that you were hurt very badly, and that hurt broke the pieces of you that stop most people from perceiving the whole world."

"There are a lot of fucked up people on this planet. Most of them don't know when there's a demon in the room."

"That's true," Mort agreed. "Maybe that's why that explanation feels unsatisfying. Because it was wrong. But the one who gave it was very wise..."

"Wisdom is overrated," Tristan said. "Maybe there's no reason for it. Maybe it just is.'"

"You could be right," Mort agreed. "I think you are."

They spent three days following the revelation doing nothing. Tristan drank and Mort sat on the porch. The noose was taken down and life seemed to settle into what Tristan hoped would be a routine. He liked having Mort around. It wasn't just the money, either. He felt much less lonely with someone else in the house. He barely noticed it anymore when the sun hit Mort's face a certain way and illuminated the skull.

Mort was so fascinated by what made Tristan able to see demons, but Tristan absolutely did not want to know what made Mort's bones seem to flash through his skin from time to time. He wasn't a demon. He was something else. Tristan didn't know what, and didn't care to know what.

He felt a yearning when he looked at Mort, a pull. A connection, maybe, though even thinking that felt like arrogance.

On the night of the third day, close to midnight, the men received another visitor. The demon appeared on the porch as a cloud slid over the moon.

Mort did not sleep. He was sitting on the couch watching wrestling on the television. It was an ancient game of good and evil he found he could relate to.

"MORT!"

Tristan startled awake when the demon shouted Mort's name.

"Keep it down," Mort hissed, banging out the screen door. He sensed Tristan's movement behind him, but wanted to deal with this uninvited visitor before Tristan fully woke up. Better to have had a bad dream than to be harassed by demons.

"Come with me."

This demon was not a lowly peon like the first messenger who had come, nor was it an ally like Balthazar. This was one of his father's enforcers, a creature who did not feel any need to be polite.

"Time to come home, boy."

The demon had thick leather bracers on his arms, and the air of a gladiator. There was no pity in his demeanor and no politeness in his tone. He was handsome in the way evil often is, brashly and boldly appealing. He had dark hair twisted into braids and tied up behind his head, dark eyes, and a prominent nose. He looked a lot like Balthazar, but without the temperance of wisdom. His dress was ancient, and standing on the porch of a modern man, he was both imposing and anachronistic.

"I'm not going anywhere," Mort said.

"You may come of your own free will, or I will drag you back. Choice is yours. For the next ten seconds."

"He doesn't want to go with you!"

Mort groaned inwardly as he turned to see Tristan staring out the window, which he had slid open to stare out, wild-eyed.

"Tris, I appreciate it, but this is not the time to get brave. This is a punisher demon."

"My name is Agamemnon."

Tristan took that information in and immediately perverted it from useful to destructive. "That's way too long a name. I'm going to call you Aggie. Go away, Aggie."

Mort's horror began to be joined by intense amusement. Tristan had woken up uncharacteristically feisty. Or perhaps it was not so uncharacteristic. Most of Tristan's tales of past malfeasance involved fighting. Perhaps now he was about to see Tristan's true colors — at the worst possible moment — which felt very on brand for Tristan.

"Not now, Tristan," he said. "Go back to sleep."

It was at that point that Tristan decided his best course of action was to climb out the window he had opened. He had relatively long limbs, so the effect was of a pale human male spidering his way into trouble.

Mort glanced at Agamemnon. He did not seem amused.

"Get off my fucking porch," Tristan said.

"Christ," Mort said, stepping between Tristan and the punisher demon. "Not now. Not here. This is not the fight you want to pick. Literally anybody else, literally any other time."

There was a rumble from the demon.

"I don't care about the mortal. You're coming with me."

"No, he's not. He's staying with me." Tristan spoke up yet again. Every time he uttered a word he made things exponentially worse.

Now he had Agamemnon's attention. "You? Who are you?"

Tristan had woken up pissed, parched, and brave. It was a feeling that had a half-life of about five minutes, and he'd used most of those first five minutes arguing with the demon at his door.

This demon had a big, thick-handled lash at his waist. Tristan's eyes were inexorably drawn to it. It looked like a thousand leather tongues attached to a handle of wood or maybe bone. He was wearing attire that looked thoroughly ancient, a skirt of sorts with thick leather tassels. His thighs were broad beneath the hem of the skirt, his calves muscular and criss-crossed with leather ties. If a guy wore a skirt around these parts, he'd be mocked relentlessly, but this demon was pulling the look off.

"I... I'm Tristan." Tristan backed slightly away from the demon. He'd never actually spoken to one before, never wanted to draw their attention. This one was bigger than the ones who had come to use his mother. He seemed more high ranking, more dangerous, probably.

"Do as you are told," the demon said. "Go back to bed."

"No!" The response was petulant and primal. Tristan regathered his courage. "You're a demon. You can't hurt me. You can't tell me what to do, and you can't tell him what to do either."

Mort palmed his face. For the first time, Tristan noticed that the kitten, always present in Mort's hood, wasn't there. That seemed like a bad sign.

"You think I cannot hurt you?" The demon's eyes flared with fire.

"You're not real," Tristan said. "I am. Go away."

For the merest fraction of a second, the demon flickered, almost as if Tristan's command had some effect.

"I'm going to hurt him." The demon spoke not to Tristan, but to Mort, informing him in a blunt, bold sort of way.

"No. Please. He doesn't know what he's doing," Mort said. "He's had enough pain in his life. You're not here for some bratty mortal. You're here for me."

Tristan felt the demon's irritation as the creature swept its gaze over him, and then over Mort, and back again.

"I see two spoiled boys, both with gifts they never had to work for, both squandering them. I should whip you both. I think I will. Starting with the mortal."

"NO!" Mort yelled, but the demon had already grabbed Tristan.

Tristan felt obsidian claws going through his clothing, brushing his skin, as he was bodily picked up by the

Punisher and carried inside his house. He fought valiantly, but there was no fight effective against this creature animated not by flesh but by sheer punitive energy.

The demon dropped him over the arm of the couch and ripped his pants from his rear, claws turning them to shreds. Tristan tried to rise, but one large clawed hand was at his back, pressing him down into the filthy cushion while behind him the other reached for the lash at his waist.

"This will teach you respect when you walk in the realms of those greater than you!" The demon intoned those words and followed them up with the harsh lash of his whip, a dozen leather tongues kissing Tristan's bare ass.

Tristan discovered in that moment that he had been completely wrong about demons. They could hurt him. He'd always thought somehow that he was untouchable, that they were like shadows, or hallucinations, not fully real. This one felt real. The big hand pressing him down felt hot and strong, and the lash it wielded stung his skin most terribly, every stroke of the lash a heavy thud followed by a swarm of stings.

"MORT!" Tristan shrieked for help. He was still fighting, but there was little he could do in this helpless, prone position.

"Leave him alone! It's me you want to hurt. He's mortal," Mort tried to argue with the demon.

"He is in as dire need of punishment as you, Prince Mortimer. Maybe more. I never get to thrash those who deserve it while they're still alive. This is a rare treat."

"Treat!?" Tristan shrieked the word as another harsh lash landed. He was being beaten like a whipping boy, taking the punishment meant for Mort. Of course, if he had stayed inside and shut up, this would never have happened, because the demon had not come for him.

Again and again, the demon's lash snapped against Tristan's poor bare flesh, leaving trails of marks, pink and red and sore. Mort seemed unable, or maybe even fucking unwilling to stop him.

"You'll think before you speak impudently to your betters, boy. And you'll consider your place in the pantheon."

"What the fuck is a pantheon!?"

It was not a long beating, but it was a thorough one. Thirteen times the Punisher's lash whipped Tristan's pale ass, while the demon excoriated Tristan's rudeness. Each and every single one of those lashes struck not only at Tristan's tender flesh, but at the core of his self. He was being humbled, brutally and methodically. He was being shown his place, and that place was lowly indeed.

When the demon was done, he used the hair at the back of Tristan's head to make him rise, meaty fingers curling into the shaggy lengths. He picked Tristan up, slapped his bare ass with his large hand, and set him on his feet.

Mort grabbed Tristan, holding him protectively close, though the protection came too late. Tristan was trying his very best not to cry, but failing as hot tears of humiliation pricked his eyes. He buried his face in Mort's neck and tried not to audibly sob.

"I'm not going with you, Agamemnon," Mort said, his lips very close to Tristan's ear. "I'm staying with him."

"Then you will be punished. The pair of you," the demon intoned. "I will be back, night after night, and if you will not come with me, he will pay the price."

"That's not fai..."

There was no chance to finish the sentence, for the Punisher had disappeared. They would see him again soon enough.

"Why did you do that?" Mort whispered the question to Tristan, holding him close. "Why did you sacrifice yourself for me?"

"I didn't mean to," Tristan wailed, letting the tears flow properly now that his tormentor was gone.

"It's okay," Mort comforted him. "The pain will fade soon, and you will feel better. Keep crying. Let it all go."

While holding the brave man who had thrown himself in the path of a demon for him, Mort must have started to feel more than just the shuddering sobs of a punished boy. He felt something else against his thigh. Something hard. A marker of arousal. When he glanced down, he saw that Tristan was rock fucking erect against his thigh.

Mort tipped Tristan's tearful face up toward him and spoke with what he hoped was gentle acceptance.

"Did you like that?"

Tristan's face flared an even brighter shade of red. "No! I don't fucking know."

"It's okay if you did," Mort said. "The ability to turn pain into pleasure can be a gift, if understood."

He wrapped his hand around Tristan's hard cock and squeezed firmly. The tears had not completely stopped, but a moan escaped Tristan's lips.

"That's right," Mort purred softly. "Let me make you feel better, my sweet, brave masochist."

He stroked Tristan's cock with slow pumps of his hand, feeling the way that part of Tristan responded to a firm touch.

"Lay back," Mort said.

"My ass hurts," Tristan whimpered. He was adorable when he was sore.

"I know. Let it hurt. It's part of the pleasure."

"What are you... what are we..."

Mort cut his questions off with a soft but firm kiss. There had been a charge between them from the beginning, but Tristan had thought he was imagining it, that Mort would never be interested in him. Nobody had ever been interested in him.

This kiss was passionate and it was calming and above all, it was trustworthy. Tristan felt himself melting into it and he did as he was told, reclining slowly.

He felt the inevitable and obvious bolt of pain as he laid back, feeling the weight of his body reignite the ache and sting of the lashes. But Mort was crouched over him this time, and his cock was engulfed first by Mort's hand, and then by his mouth.

"Fuck!" Tristan cursed as he felt himself being sucked by a hot, wet void. Mort's lips were tight around his cock, and his fingers skillfully stroked Tristan's balls.

The latent confusion of this sudden physical confession of mutual desire kept Tristan from fully sinking into the sensation for a moment or two, then he gave in. The feelings were so good, so intense. He felt deep energy, long denied, being released and flowing through his body, twirling down his spine. Mort sucked him like he loved him, with an energy and a desire that obliterated any thought in Tristan's head.

Mort stroked and sucked, cajoling and then commanding orgasm. Tristan had always thought of the act of sucking dick to be submissive, but somehow Mort made it an entirely dominant act. Tristan laid back and let himself be made to feel good, comforted, pleasured, and finally, released.

"FUCK!" Tristan roared as his hips jerked and a stream of seed escaped his cock and filled Mort's mouth.

Mort swallowed every drop of cum and sat up between Tristan's legs with a smile.

"Feel better?"

"God, you're fucking good at that," Tristan said when he could finally breathe. His ass still hurt, but his head felt clear. He was doing better, a lot better than he had before.

"I just wanted to make you feel good. You deserve pleasure as much as you deserve pain."

"I deserve pain?"

"Well." Mort smirked just a little. "You did refuse to do as you were told by both of us. You earned that whipping. Agamemnon wouldn't have looked at you twice if you hadn't gone out of your way to get his attention. Calling him Aggie," Mort snorted. "You were lucky to get off with a whipping. I think he liked you."

"Liked me? I don't fucking think so. I pissed him off."

"True, but sadists always have a soft spot for masochists intent on deserving punishment," Mort said.

"What are you?" Tristan changed the subject and put the spotlight back on Mort. "I mean, really. Demons are coming for you, demanding you go back. But you don't look like a demon to me. You don't act like one, either. So...."

Mort gave a little shrug.

"So you're, what, a demon?"

"Not quite," Mort said. "I'm..." He thought for a second. "I'm more like a delivery guy."

Tristan laughed. "Some fucking delivery guy. What do you deliver?"

"Souls."

Two and two came together and made four.

"So you came, that day... you came to... take me..."

"I had already quit. I was not coming to take you. I suppose you could say I simply found you."

"I'm glad you did," Tristan said.

"Are you? Even though I just got your ass whipped by a punisher demon?"

"I probably deserved it," Tristan said, displaying greater insight than usual. His head felt a lot clearer than it had in a long time. Some of that was because of the fucking awesome orgasm Mort had just given him, and some of it was from the pain the Punisher had dealt.

"Well, arguably," Mort smiled. "We have a problem, though. Agamemnon is going to return. He will come back night after night, or if not him, someone else. They will never let me stay here."

Tristan thought about that for a long moment. Mort was sitting next to him on the couch, their legs entangled in casual new intimacy. Then, an idea came to him, an idea so perfect it made him smile slowly.

"What?" Mort said, his tone slightly wary. "I don't know if I like that look on your face."

"If they won't accept your resignation," Tristan said. "Maybe it's time you got fired." He yawned deeply.

"Maybe it's time you got some sleep," Mort said in turn. "You must be exhausted."

6

Tristan slept most of the day, which was his habit anyway if he wasn't disturbed, and woke around six o'clock in the evening. He felt a certain amount of excitement and anticipation as he clambered out of bed. Most of his life he had been a fuck up, and fucking up had never done him or anybody else any good. Now, though, it was going to save a friend.

"Mort? Mort! MORT!"

"I'm in the kitchen," Mort said calmly. "It's mere feet from where you're standing."

"Right," Tristan said, poking his scruffy blond head around the door with a rakish grin. "Are you ready to hear my plan to get this whole problem sorted?"

Mort was sitting in a kitchen chair, his long legs extended under the table, sunset light starting to gleam across his face. There was a hint of skull, cheekbone and teeth, for a moment. Tristan blinked and it was gone.

He charged over to the table, putting both hands on it, leaning forward with an almost feral excitement. He'd usually have sat down, but his ass hurt. Because a demon had given him a beating. That humiliation would not go unavenged.

"Alright, so, you're already doing the first thing you need to do to get fired. You stopped showing up. Usually that's enough. But sometimes, like this time, they work out a way to force you back into work. And that's when you go to step two. Being a huge fuck up."

Mort's smile was indulgent.

"I appreciate the inspiration, really, I do. And I am sure you have plenty of experience. But I am a conductor of souls, and that is not something one can just fuck up."

"Why not?"

"People are relying on me."

"So?"

"It's too important a job to fuck up." Mort's expression was attractively serious. There was an air about him now that Tristan had not fully appreciated before, a beautiful solemnity.

"Is that why you quit?"

"I quit because..." Mort pressed his lips together as if he did not want to speak the next word out of his mouth. "I quit."

"Alright. Then we execute plan B. You continue to quit. I make the demons' lives a living hell if they don't leave you alone."

"Uh huh," Mort smiled, relaxing a little. "I'd love to see how you plan to make a demon's life hell."

"Easy. I die, and then I go to Hell and I just... fuck with them."

"Alright," Mort sighed. "Let's try a plan where you stay alive."

"Okay. If you want. But dead or alive, I owe you my life. So."

Tristan looked earnestly at Mort for a second before dropping his eyes. That was about all the emotional intensity he could stand before his morning beer.

"I'll do what I have to. Or whatever," Tristan said.

He felt Mort's dark gaze on him. "You are very sweet, but you owe me nothing. You have given me a place to stay."

"You could stay anywhere. You could buy a whole fucking house. You don't need me."

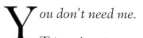

Y*ou don't need me.*

Tristan's voice cracked in the last part of the sentence in a way that made parts of Mort melt.

Seeing Tristan bent for the Punisher had been one of the most erotically charged experiences of Mort's existence. Mort had not been made for connection, or carnal experiences, but in this mortal plane he found himself capable of all sorts of things. Lust was one of them, but this was more than lust. This was connection. When he was with Tristan, he felt a kind of attachment that made even hearing the mention of Tristan's potential demise painful.

He reached out and put a hand over Tristan's hand. "I need you."

"Cool," Tristan said, hiding his feelings behind a taciturn veil. It wasn't a rejection, though it might have looked like one to a layman.

Mort noticed that Tristan had not immediately gone for a beer. It was the first time in their association that he had not reached for that lifeline immediately upon waking.

The delay did not last any longer than Mort's rejection of his plans, though. The refrigerator door opened with a familiar squeal, followed by the sound of a tab being pulled.

Tristan leaned against the counter, threw his head back, and gulped at the beer. He was shirtless, as usual. The rippling of his stomach muscles in the evening light was entrancing. Tristan was many things, but most of all he was alive. Vibrantly, rebelliously alive.

"Why did you want to kill yourself?" Suddenly, Mort had to know the answer to the question.

Tristan snorted into the now empty can before lowering it. "As if I needed a reason."

Mort could tell he was being evasive, and Tristan could tell that Mort could tell.

"Why did you quit delivering souls?" Tristan threw the question back at him.

Mort pressed his lips together.

"Maybe it's best we keep our secrets for now."

"Yeah," Tristan said with a pointed look. "Maybe."

"I'm sorry. I didn't mean to pry."

"It's fine. It's... you don't know what it's like to have a life," Tristan said. "It's supposed to be one thing, but it's never that thing. You have all these hopes and dreams when you're a kid, and people encourage them. They say you can be anything. But the truth is, you're going to be whatever you're going to be. People don't get as many choices as they think they do."

He took a deep breath, as if he was finished, then he started up again.

"They tell us we can be anything, and then they do everything in their power to make us nothing. You have to play the game. Their game. You have to be respectable. You have to be safe. You have to follow rules." He looked at Mort, his eyes lit with passion. "There's no life left in life anymore. There's not even survival. There's just something in the middle, some... pointless, gray, meaningless fucking expanse that is too long and too short at the same time."

Mort loved Tristan so fiercely in that moment he could barely handle it. He pushed back the chair, stood up, grabbed his mortal lover by the chin and pressed a kiss of pure passion to Tristan's lips.

He tasted Tristan. Tasted the beer, the sadness, and the anger. Tasted the wasted potential, and the grief. Mortality was so cruel and so beautiful, and he tasted that too.

"I know exactly what you mean," he said when he broke the kiss. "You are so beautiful, and the life you are living does not reflect that. You don't see it in the mirrors of your home, or in the world. But if you could see what I see, you would understand that you are the most incredible creature as far as any eye can see."

"Fuck," Tristan blushed.

"I don't mean to frighten you. I know I am intense. And I know what we did last night was a fresh intimacy. But I want you to know now, while you have the chance to know, that you are loved."

Tristan was stunned. Absolutely fucking stunned.

"Uh. Uhm. Er. I'm, uhm, loved? By.... you?"

Mort's smile was soft. "Yes, Tristan. By me. I love you."

"Well, fuck," Tristan said. He didn't know what to say to that. Definitely didn't know how to accept it, let alone process it, let alone return the sentiment.

Mort's smile let him off the hook. "I don't need you to say it back. It's not an obligation. I just want you to know, because it's important."

"Do you think that demon will come back?" Tristan changed the subject.

～

Aside from the confusing confession of love, whatever that meant practically, Tristan couldn't stop thinking about the Punisher. What he had done, what he hadn't done. What Tristan had thought and felt while it was all happening. He didn't want it to happen again. He didn't want to feel all the shame he'd felt in his life concentrated under the lash or palm of some stranger, a creature that only existed to bring pain to those who deserved it.

He knew he was a pathetic creature, and he knew he deserved to hurt. He was fairly certain he didn't deserve the pleasure Mort had brought him after. And he was absolutely sure he did not deserve Mort's love.

Instead of processing any of that, Tristan did what generations of men in his family had presumably done before him: he worked out somebody to blame and something to kill.

"I think something will eventually come," Mort said. "It might be better if you were not here when it does. So far, our guests have been benign, but eventually my father will send less temperate mercenaries to persuade me back to work."

"We go on the offensive then."

"You mean I should not do my work even harder?"

Tristan smiled, and the smile was reckless. "I can see demons. And last night, one touched me."

"Did more than touch you, but yes, I understand."

"If they can touch me, I can touch them."

Mort caught his drift immediately and was not encouraging.

"Have you ever won a single fight you've ever been in, Tris?"

"No. But there's always a first time."

"Not against a demon, there isn't. Don't try to fight what may come. Stay out of the way. I can handle myself."

Tristan felt himself grabbed, one cold hand at the back of his head, and pulled into a kiss. This time it wasn't just a kiss of passion, though there was still that charge. This time, it was a kiss of dominance. A *do what I say* kind of kiss. What Mort got back was a *make me* kind of moan, but Mort didn't seem to pick up on that.

7

Though he didn't argue at the time, Tristan had no intention of staying out of the way. He had never been loved before, and there was no way he was going to let the forces of Hell snatch away the one person who loved him.

He was going to keep Mort. He had experience clinging to death, and he had a lot of experience causing chaos. He would do whatever it took to keep Mort in his life.

Nobody came that night. Or the next night, but that was fine with Tristan because it gave him time to move things into place.

Mort thought Tristan was tidying the house, and he was, in a way. He was constructing defenses based on designs long ago downloaded from the Internet back in the 1990's, when the recipes of anarchists were freely available.

Mort didn't ask a lot of questions, because Mort wasn't a person, not really, and Mort didn't have typical human curiosity. For all he knew, it was quite normal for someone to be creating small caches of metallic objects.

"So," Tristan said. "Demons. Do they have any weaknesses? Like vampires are supposed to be afraid of crosses?"

"Demons are made of many different things, and depending on what they are made of, they may be sensitive to certain things, but..."

Tristan almost zoned out while listening to Mort's non-explanation.

"Demons aren't made for the mortal realm. They come for me because I am not made for it either. They are beings of energy. The Punisher punished you because you have so much latent energy, Tris. You're so strong. But it makes them strong against you too."

"So I make them more physical, and then they're vulnerable to physical things?"

"In a way... What are you up to?" Mort's gaze and tone had both become quite sharp.

"Learning," Tristan said. "I can't stay stupid forever."

"You have never been stupid." Mort lowered his head a little and gave Tristan a stern stare. "Neither have I."

"Uh huh. Awesome. Aren't we a pair of smart boys."

Tristan was in a better mood than Mort had ever seen him. He'd only had one beer that day, enough to stave off tremors and other unpleasant side effects of alcohol withdrawal. It was a significant decrease of his usual consumption, which saw at least two six packs being drained down his throat. He was looking sharper, more motivated. He'd even taken a shower and put on a fresh pair of jeans. Still no shirt, which Mort was fine with. He enjoyed looking at the rippling abdominals of his chosen human mate.

Tristan was gathering fireworks now, old fireworks. He was peeling the bright paper off the sides of them and dumping the interior into little paper canisters. He seemed very happy in this task, which Mort still imagined was tidying. Tristan's hair had been brushed back wet against his head and there was an expression on his face of appealing intensity.

Tristan had been reorganizing the house a lot lately. Mort did not understand the significance of many of the choices he made. Dishes were usually stacked in cupboards, for instance, while cutlery went in drawers. Both of those protocols made about as much sense as firework powder being removed from fireworks and stockpiled in larger containers. Sometimes mortals moved things from big containers to small, other times they moved things from small containers to big.

At one point, Tristan even began cutting not just the plastic rings from the beer cans, but the beer cans themselves, turning the shining silver cylinders into much smaller, irregularly-shaped pieces which he swept quite carefully into a cardboard box. Even to Mort's inexperienced gaze it was a strange kind of tidying, but it was something that seemed to keep him occupied.

Mort liked seeing Tristan happy, and resolved not to interfere in whatever he was doing.

That turned out to be a significant mistake.

~

lip... clop...

Later that evening, another demon did come. This time it was not a Punisher. It was an Enforcer. Hell was escalating through the ranks, with the notable exception of Balthazar, who was above rank and had come of his own accord. Tristan and Mort heard hooves on the porch, too heavy and too large to belong to anything smaller than a horse.

It wasn't a horse, though it was built like a bull, albeit with the head and face of a man. This big red muscular demon was here for one reason and one reason alone.

To Mort's dismay Tristan flashed to the window as soon as he heard the steps, peering out between the old fly-marked blinds. What he saw should have terrified him. That would have been a natural mortal response, but Tristan didn't have a natural mortal response to anything.

Mort heard Tristan utter words under his breath, an excited little *fuck yeah*. Mort didn't like them, but he hadn't known Tristan long enough to know just how worrying those words were.

"MORT!" The Enforcer shouted Mort's name. "I come to deliver you to your father's kingdom to answer for your insubordination!"

Tristan slid the window open and stuck his head out into the porch. Right into the physical space of the big red demon.

"Hey, buddy, fuck off."

Tristan was absolutely spoiling for a fight, or was it punishment? Tristan probably couldn't tell the difference between a Punisher and an Enforcer. He didn't know what he was doing. He just knew that he was getting into trouble.

Mort felt something inside him starting to grow, an opposing force to Tristan's recklessness.

"Get inside," he said. He didn't usually speak to Tristan so bluntly, or with so much authority, but this was getting dangerous and he did not want to see his mortal mate hurt.

"No. This asshole is on my porch, so he gets my fucking words."

Tristan did not have a submissive bone in his body. Tristan was disobedient. Of course his first reaction was to refuse to obey. Mort felt the fingers of his right hand flexing with the urge to take Tristan in hand, but there wasn't time for that now.

The Enforcer demon was determined to lay his hands on Mort and drag him to the underworld. That, Mort could not allow. The asking-nicely-and-waiting-patiently phase of affairs had well and truly ended. Now they were in the being-forced-against-your-will phase. Mort had known this was coming, but it seemed Tristan had sensed it too — and it was Tristan's sense of the thing that turned out to be the most dangerous element of the situation.

The Enforcer was not going to wait on the porch. The Enforcer was going to push through the front door and come inside.

Tristan, it seemed, had been counting on that.

Mort prepared to banish the beast, but before he could do anything, Tristan's plans unfurled in all their glorious carnage. The demon came through the front door, identifying it as the obvious point of entry. It was not locked. It had not been locked in years. If there was a key, Mort had never seen it and he doubted Tristan knew where it was.

There was nothing to stop the demon from walking right into Tristan's home. And absolutely nothing stopping the massive foul beast from regretting that decision immediately.

The second the door opened, heretofore nearly invisible strands of fishing wire were pulled taut, starting an incendiary cascade of great inventiveness and even greater damage.

The entire room exploded, or rather, imploded into a metal trap. The motion of the demon coming through the door triggered gunpowder reservoirs in multiple locations throughout the house, each of those shells detonating what could only be described as a directed dirty bomb of twisted cheap cutlery, shredded old beer cans, screws, widgets, and the entire contents of the junk drawer. All the bits and pieces Tristan and his mother had put away over the years thinking they would one day be useful were suddenly in use.

The demon shrieked in shock as its body was absolutely pummeled with bits of sharp things. It had not expected to be wounded, or to suffer physical damage of any kind. It had probably never been hurt in all its many thousands of years of existence as a construct of the afterworld. But now it bled. Bits of it were on the ground, ripped away by the harsh spray of mortal debris.

Tristan didn't just see demons. He solidified them. He made them real in a way they had not been real before. He manifested them.

All of these thoughts flashed through Mort's mind in quick succession as he stepped forward and used his power to banish the wounded and now thoroughly frightened demon.

"BEGONE! I BANISH AND BIND YOU TO THE NETHER REALMS, YOU AND YOUR KIND, FOREVER AND EVER..."

The demon screamed and disappeared, turning from flesh to mist in an instant. It was a merciful escape from the harsh and swift torture Tristan had inflicted on it. Mort never liked to see suffering.

"*Amen...*" Tristan gasped the word.

There was something in the quality of the tone of Tristan's voice that worried Mort immediately. He swung around to see Tristan on the floor, bleeding from many places.

The trap had been successful. Too successful. The spray of household shrapnel had caught the left side of Tristan. He was pale where he was not red, his hands trembling as he tried to staunch the flow of his many wounds.

Mort slid to his knees in the growing pool of Tristan's blood.

"What have you done? Why?" He lifted Tris' head and cradled it tenderly in his lap. The kitten emerged from its hiding place behind the sofa and took up sphinx-like residence at the edge of the blood, occasionally lapping a little.

"I killed the demon." In spite of his pain, Tristan had the nerve to seem proud of that, even though it was not in any way true.

"You've nearly killed yourself. How did I not see what you were doing? Why was I not more suspicious of you cutting the tines off every fork in the house and stuffing them into a bag around a..."

Tristan coughed up a little blood. "Pretty stupid, bro," he choked out.

Mort wanted to lecture him, wanted to kiss him, wanted to beat him, wanted to tie him up for his own damn good, but he could do none of those things. Tristan was going to die if Mort did not do something to preserve his life, but Mort had absolutely no idea how to save a mortal life. His expertise lay in the other side of that particular coin.

He needed help.

8

Tom woke up to find himself being dragged out of bed by a blood-soaked specter of death. This set off all sorts of screaming, begging, and pleading that Mort was quite used to, but had no time for.

"Where is the nearest hospital?" Mort questioned him, well aware that in this light, the full skull shade of his face was showing. He did not appear in any way mortal in this moment.

"Uh...uh...." Tom wore a volunteer firefighter t-shirt that clung to his biceps, and tight boxers that left nothing to the imagination.

"The hospital," Mort repeated. "Where?"

Tom babbled something about north and west and left and right, and in the end Mort just dragged him out of the house, threw him in the passenger seat of his own car and forbade him to move. His reaper qualities guaranteed submission and obedience from Tom. If only they had the same effect on Tristan, there would be no need for any of this.

"Tell me where to go."

Tom looked over his shoulder, to where Tristan was slowly bleeding out in the back seat. That seemed to wake him up.

"Let me get back there," he said. "I can put pressure on the wounds, and I can tell you where the hospital is."

"Alright. Good. Thank you."

Tom squirmed through the front seats and got to Tristan in the back. Tom was competent at fixing trucks. Mort hoped he was as competent at first aid.

T ristan survived long enough to make it to the hospital in Perdition.

Mort was familiar with hospitals. When he had worked, he was there all the time. They took Tristan right away, which even Mort knew was a bad sign. If he had been working, he would have been able to melt through the people and be by Tristan's side. As it was, his presence in the mortal realm had begun to make him solid and subject to the laws of mortals.

"Sit down, sir."

"I want to see my friend."

"Sit down, sir," the nurse repeated. She was tired, over-worked, and underpaid. There were dark circles under her eyes, and a pinched look around her mouth. She did not have time for anybody's bullshit. Not even Death himself could have intimidated her. She was far too used to it.

Tom reached up, grabbed Mort's arm, and pulled him down into one of the plastic chairs arranged in dour rows throughout the waiting room.

All around them, he heard the sick and felt the dying. It felt oddly comforting, like being back home.

"What the fuck happened to him?" Tom asked the question.

"He created some sort of a..." Mort was momentarily lost for words. "A trap, with the innards of fireworks and pieces of metal, cut up beer cans."

"Fucking idiot," Tom cursed. "He was always a fucking moron."

"Don't talk about him that way."

"Sorry," Tom said, his skin going to goosebumps with the sudden chill that came with Mort's disapproval. "But it's true."

Not so sorry, then.

Tristan had not earned the respect of his peers because Tristan always did whatever he wanted to do, regardless of whether or not it made sense or would work. He had absolutely no regard for his own life, and probably had not in years. To others, that instability read as being untrustworthy and dangerous.

"He is not stupid. He is incredibly inventive and intelligent. What he is not, is careful."

"I remember Tristan making wings out of plastic bags in like, fifth grade. He said an angel told him how to make them, and he was going to fly. He jumped off a water tower and broke both his legs. My mom said he'd probably be taken away because social services knew he didn't have a daddy and his momma was a wh..." Tom paused and corrected himself, trying to make his speech more respectful. "His momma was a hooker."

Swing and a miss.

"And did they come?"

"Sure, they came one day. Tristan ran away, wouldn't let them take him. Everybody thought he fucking died out in the desert. Was gone for forty days. Then bam, one day, he walks into class like nothing happened. It was wild."

"Forty days?"

"Forty days and forty nights," Tom nodded. "Biblical shit."

It was, indeed, biblical shit.

Mort learned many things from Tom that night, uppermost among them, that Tristan had always been a handful, and he had always been a survivor. So why in hell had he been trying to string a noose when Mort met him?

Someone in the chair behind him coughed, rustled a paper, and leaned in far too close for politeness or comfort.

"Fancy meeting you here, cousin."

Anubis.

Nobody else in the waiting room saw the jackal's face, but Mort was treated to the sleek, dark snout and even darker, mocking eyes.

"What brings you to the hospital, Mort? Can't be the poor souls slipping from their physical bodies, can it. You don't do that kind of work anymore. Is it the one you tried to save? How is that going?"

Anubis was smug.

"Great," Mort said. "Wonderful."

He was glad for their conversation to be interrupted by the arrival of a harried-looking doctor.

"Are you two with Tristan Stevens?"

"Yeah," Tom said. "That's us."

Mort did not dare speak, lest his true nature be revealed. Doctors and medical staff had an uncanny way of picking him out sometimes. Not because they saw demons like Tristan did, but because their work took them repeatedly to the very lines between life and death.

"Your friend is going to survive," the doctor said. "He's lost a lot of blood, but we are replacing that. If either one of you would like to make a donation to help replenish our stores, that would be appreciated."

Tom was already rolling a nonexistent sleeve up. "Sure, boss. Where do I go?"

"To the clinic during open hours. It's three in the morning."

"Oh. Right."

"Appreciate your willingness, though. You can take him home once the transfusions are done," the doctor said. "And don't let him do whatever it was he did again. Technically, I should be reporting him to the police, but frankly, I don't need the paperwork."

Hell had demons. Humans had paperwork.

9

"You're mad at me."

Mort hadn't spoken since they'd gotten back home. Tristan was propped up on the couch, covered in bandages and wounds that would be scars soon enough. There was one particularly deep one on his left cheek that had taken thirty stitches to close. That wasn't ever going to go away.

Tristan didn't care about the scars, or the pain, or even the fact he wasn't allowed beer on the doctor's orders, and Mort had thrown it all out on arrival. He did care that Mort wouldn't talk to him. He was starting to freak out.

"Are you... just going to bounce, or what the fuck?"

It wasn't the most diplomatic way of asking the question, but Tristan wasn't the most diplomatic sort of guy.

Mort was sitting at the kitchen table, looking out the window, just a hint of skull shining in daylight. When he turned to look at Tristan, shadow covered his very handsome, very human-looking visage. He was breathtakingly beautiful and solemn and Tristan felt so keenly in that moment that he absolutely did not deserve a man like this. Mort was far more than a man. He was a psycho... something. He was supernatural. And he had no fucking reason to be here. So it made sense that he'd leave.

"You almost died," Mort said.

"So? What does it matter?"

That was the wrong thing to say. Tristan saw pure rage build on Mort's face. It took several minutes for Mort to contain himself enough to speak.

"It is a one way trip," Mort said. "If you die, you and I would not be reunited. You would forget everything about your life, including me."

"I could never forget you."

"You could never remember me. You wouldn't have a mind, boy."

Tristan frowned at that piece of news, and at the moniker he'd been given. Not Tristan or the more familiar Tris. *Boy.*

"Did you just call me boy?"

"Yes. I did. Because that is what you are."

"You think I'm some spoiled little shit who..."

"You have never been spoiled a day in your life," Mort interrupted, standing up to walk over to Tristan. He leaned down, one hand on the arm of the couch, the other pressed against the cushion next to Tristan's head, boxing him in. They were practically the same height, but in that moment

Tristan felt like Mort was twice his size at least. The dark gaze of death's deliverer seared into his soul.

"You have been neglected, bullied, abused, and degraded," Mort said. "You have been led to believe that you are worthless, and so you treat yourself as if you do not matter... Tristan!"

Tristan's eyes snapped back to Mort's, as he forced Tristan to meet his dark gaze with a sharp utterance of his name. "I call you boy because that is what you are to me. You are my boy. Understand? MINE."

Tristan lowered his head in shame, and to avoid the intensity of the moment. Mort did not allow it.

The reaper's fingers took hold of his chin and tipped his head back, carefully angling it so Tristan met his dark gaze. There was no escaping him. "But you are only mine as long as you live. Which means you have to live, Tristan. Completely, fully, and for a long time. Do you understand?"

Tristan allowed himself the smallest of nods. He was in trouble, but not the kind of trouble he was used to, the kind that got him rejected and made an outcast. This was a different kind of trouble. A trouble that pulled Mort closer and gave Tristan nowhere to hide. He felt very guilty, very ashamed, and very small. All those feelings were clearly evident in his nearly squeaked response.

"Yes, sir."

He'd never called anybody sir in his entire life, but now felt like a good time to start.

Mort got fucking hard when Tristan called him sir. It meant so much more coming from the lips of a man who never allowed anybody else the satisfaction of feeling better than him. Tristan was usually a scrap it out, bring 'em down to his level sort of guy.

He didn't want to be distracted by how hot Tristan was right now. He wanted to make sure he'd been understood. Truly. Deeply.

Tristan was trying, but Mort had the feeling he wouldn't get it for a while. Not really. He was mistaking insight for pity, thinking that there was something wrong with him.

"I'll do anything..." Tristan whimpered. "Just don't go."

"I'm not going anywhere," Mort said firmly.

He knew this wasn't going to be easy. Tristan had no idea how to be obedient. He didn't follow laws, he just managed not to break them out of coincidence most of the time. He was a law unto himself, and that meant he had a lot to learn about submission.

It might very well not be possible, Mort considered, running bone fingers through blond locks. Some creatures were dominant, most were submissive. Most people he had encountered were looking for a leader. But perhaps even in those who craved a dominant figure, the ability to trust had been so very broken it was impossible for them to let themselves surrender. Tristan might be one of those theoretical people. And if he was, what could Mort do? He was painfully aware that he was not God. He could not bring life. He could only bring death, and death would be the end of Tristan.

There was probably no controlling Tris. But there might be some way of making a bargain with a different devil.

Tristan woke up in pain, pain he was happy to bear because it meant he was alive. Mort's words had cut deep the previous day, and they were still on his mind. Death was an end. Not an end of soul, but an end of memory. The implications of that were intense. If the dead did not remember, then...

He suddenly found himself very keen to cling to his memories. To his self. To the very parts of his being that he had been so keen to discard like trash. To the here and the now.

He found himself wanting life.

The kitten was tucked beneath his nose. It never seemed to grow. It was still small and fuzzy and adorable, and it meant that Mort was not far away.

"Mort?"

He called for his... lover? Not really. One *sorry I got you beaten* blowjob didn't really qualify them as lovers.

Mort came into the room obligingly. He was tall and dark and strong. He also looked solemn, but that was his expression in general. For once, Tristan was fairly certain he hadn't done anything wrong. He had been asleep, and even he couldn't fuck that up.

"I was worried you were gone," Tristan said, hearing how small he sounded.

"I am not gone, but I do need to take a little trip. I won't be long. I will be back before dinner, certainly."

"Where are you going?"

"I cannot risk your life again," Mort said. "I am going to see my father."

"Oh," Tristan said. "Say hi to your dad for me."

Mort was absolutely not going to say hi to his dad for Tristan. Mort's father was great and deep and dark, formless. He was the void itself, the space between things.

Mort stood at the last bit of thingness and made his sacrifice.

"I will make a deal," he said. "I will give you the rest of eternity, if you will give me the lifetime of this mortal."

His father took form in the guise of a human skeleton many miles tall. It was in this form he conversed with his wayward son. He spoke with knowledge of all things, for he saw all.

"When you met this human, he had minutes left. You would trade all eternity for one unstable human male who courts death so eagerly? You might have days, hours, perhaps minutes — not years."

"I would exchange all eternity for one day with him."

His father laughed, not cruelly, and not indulgently, but somewhere in between. And then he did something he probably considered merciful.

"I will not accept this deal, because you are not thinking clearly. You have allowed yourself to be drawn into mortal psychodrama, and it will destroy you. Your pledge of eternity will mean nothing if you become as they are."

Mort's father loved him. Wanted him to exist. That was the most basic and primal functions of love, to create and preserve existence. It was the love of a parent for a child, and the love Mort was beginning to understand he had for his boy.

Mort's father continued speaking. "He loves you because you are an end, and he desperately seeks an end. He yearns for me, for unbecoming. These are all releases from his prison of flesh. He does not appreciate his life, and he can never appreciate you, my son. Not as anything more than a whisper of what he most craves."

"You don't know him."

"I have known many like him. I contain many like him."

For a moment, the illusion of the great skeleton parted, and in its place swarmed a myriad of what some would call lost souls. They were lost no longer. They were at home.

Mort felt what might be the weight and truth of his father's words. He wanted to reject them. Needed to push them away. But they had already infected him. They had found the little seeds of doubt deep inside him, and they had made him wonder if Tristan's love was not love at all, but merely part of his compulsion for an end.

"I know I cannot tell you what to do. I did not make you to obey. I made you because souls need guides. You are one of the very few creatures in existence to truly have a purpose.

You were made for something. The mortals you encounter, they were not made for anything."

Mort's gut rebelled against that statement, but he could make no good argument against it, and it was not why he was there.

"I will let that purpose dictate events," his father said. "I will not attempt to force you back to your work. Your work will lure you, however, because it is what you were made for."

"If that's true, why did you send the Punisher and the Enforcer? Why send anyone at all?"

"I wanted you to know that you were missed."

Mort sighed, though he did not need to breathe. This was another of his father's games.

"Go back to your mortal," his father said. "You are what you are. He is what he is, and what will be, will be. I will not send demons to pursue you. The boy you have chosen contains multitudes of his own."

Mort felt a cold, creeping sense of inevitability as he returned to the mortal realm. His father was never wrong. About anything.

Hope had been drained by the paternal visit. He wondered what he was going back to. More suicidal behavior, either deliberate or shaded in the clothing of accidents. More hopeless struggling against the inevitability of what Tristan seemed to want more than he wanted anything else.

He needed to understand Tristan's pain so he could understand how to help him, not to mention why he was drawn to him. There was a connection between them, a thread that had drawn Mort inexorably the moment he laid down the burden of his purpose. He needed to understand that too.

As he came up the porch stairs and stepped in through the screen door, he found the house filled with light from the bright desert afternoon. Tristan was standing with a pan in hand. The kitchen was coated in a fine white powder.

What have you done now? The thought ran through Mort's head, as he made the assumption that once again things were going wrong. When he saw Tristan and a mess, he braced himself for unpleasantness.

The air smelled sweet, not sickly, but pleasantly so. There was a sound too, a sizzling. Was he cooking?

"You're back!" Tristan seemed excited about that. "I made pancakes. I was hungry. Haven't felt hungry in a long time. I think it's not drinking. Makes all the other body systems sort of get active, you know?"

Mort did not know, but he felt some of the cold of the underworld melt from his bones. The dreadful prophecy felt much less real now in the face of Tristan's energy. His father did not know everything. He knew what had happened, not what would yet happen. He was a creature of history, not of the future.

Tristan smiled at Mort, or at least attempted to with his face stitched up, his eyes bright and clear.

"I've been thinking about what you said. And you're right. I've got this life, I might as well start living it. I mean, I was living it. But..." He looked into Mort's eyes. "It's different with you around."

"The demons won't be coming anymore," Mort said. That felt like an important piece of news to impart.

"So you told your dad where to go? Good for you, man. Good for you."

Tris flipped a pancake onto a plate and offered it to Mort.

Mort ate it, savoring the experience of consuming something Tristan had made for him.

"I wanted to ask you something," Tristan said, smearing his hands on his jeans.

"Oh?"

Mort wanted to ask Tristan many things, but he didn't let that be known. He made space for the bright mortal before him, whose very presence chased shadows away.

"So. Uhm. Are you. Into me?"

The way Tristan asked the question, so uncertain, yet so brave, made Mort melt. He leaned against the kitchen counter and looked into Tristan's eyes as much as he could. Tristan was trying to hide again behind an increasingly long shock of shaggy hair.

"I told you I love you," he reminded him.

"Yeah. I know. But like, my mom loved me. She wasn't into me. Which was a good thing, but I'm asking you... are you......"

"Into you," Mort finished his sentence when it had hung on too long.

"Sexually," Tristan clarified, brave in the face of awkwardness.

"Yes," Mort said, putting him out of his misery, as he had been designed to do. "I am into you. Sexually."

"Cool. Cool. So uh, we haven't..."

"It hasn't been... appropriate. I found you trying to do something so destructive you would not have survived it."

"Sure, I was in a bad way, but I'm better now."

Mort smiled at Tristan's impatience. Barely twenty-four hours ago he had been getting his face sewn back together.

"You haven't had time to recover from anything."

"Really? Feels like long enough."

"In a matter of days you have tried to kill yourself and almost been killed by a demon. Intimacy of the kind you and I desire is not... appropriate."

"Because I am damaged?" Tristan immediately made it about his shortcomings, as Mort knew he would. Tristan made an escape from the stove to the kitchen table, carrying a stack of pancakes on a bright yellow plate. Mort turned to follow him.

"Because I want to be careful with you," he said as Tristan sat down.

"Aw," Tristan said, leaning the good side of his face on his hand and smiling at Mort. He was charming when he wanted to be, and also sometimes when he didn't want to be.

"And because we have all the time in this world. Assuming you manage to stay in it."

Mort could feel Anubis nearby. His cousin had taken his territory, one psychopomp covering for another. The people of northwest Nevada would be surprised to meet an Egyptian god when they passed. It would be an interesting twist in the last part of their various tales. Mort didn't mind about the rest of them, but Anubis would gloat if he had the chance to take Tris. He would be insufferable, and Mort would be inconsolable.

"I'm going to stay in this world," Tristan said. "I'm not giving that dog the fucking satisfaction."

"Dog?"

"Yeah. A German Shepherd at the hospital. Walked on his hind legs, sniffing around. He came and stood at the end of my bed while they stitched me up, giving me this goofy fucking look."

Anubis would not like being described as a German Shepherd. Or goofy, for that matter. But that was how these things worked. Psychopomps were perceived through the eyes of those who beheld them. He'd forgotten about that part. Maybe the people of northwest Nevada would find themselves escorted by a plain ol' doggie.

As Tristan described the scene there was an expression of distaste on his face that Mort found very appealing, given it was in reference to Anubis.

"Tom told me something." Mort changed the subject. "He said that you once ran away into the desert for forty days."

"Oh. Yeah. That was a long time ago." Tris scratched at one of his bandages. He was already healing. He was strong. Stronger than anybody who abused his body as much as he did had any right to be.

"You were a child," Mort nodded. "I've seen these deserts. Walked through them. There are few, close to no water sources, and even less food."

"I made do."

"Apparently. But I have to wonder how."

Tristan's smile faded slightly. He shifted in his chair. An expression of something like guilt flashed over his face. "I don't know," he said, lying terribly. He hadn't lied to Mort before, and Mort found that he did not like it one bit.

"There are devils in the desert," Mort said, keeping his tone casual. "It would be easy to strike a deal with one, if you were young, desperate, and dying."

"Are you accusing me of something?" Tristan cut into the stack of pancakes with his fork, then shoved them into his mouth.

"No. I am just wondering if that might have been where your gift of seeing demons comes from."

"Saw them before that," Tristan said. "You want some of these?" He leaned back in his chair, precariously putting the old wood structure on two back legs instead of four as he reached backwards for a fork on the counter. He couldn't do the most simple of things without making the act a danger to himself.

He swung back, unharmed, and the muscles in his arm rippled pleasingly as he offered Mort a fork.

It was impossible to be angry at Tristan or stay serious around him. He was such a study in contradictions. Sometimes he was so maudlin, so self-destructive, yearning for annihilation. And other times he made pancakes and tried to get laid.

"Thank you..." Mort said, taking the fork from Tristan, and taking a seat next to him. "... boy." He added the affectionate moniker and watched, pleased, as Tristan blushed around a mouthful of pancake.

"When you call me that, it fucks with me," Tristan observed, ever the one to speak his internal monologue out loud.

Mort smiled. "Good."

"Good, you like fucking with me? Or maybe you want to just straight up fuck me?"

Words spoken with a hopeful grin made Mort smile in return.

"If you can be good boy, I might fuck your mouth."

Tristan's eyes hooded with longing. "And if I'm a bad boy?"

"Well..." Mort purred. "Then I'd have to punish you, wouldn't I?"

An even broader grin spread over Tristan's face. He tried to hide it but failed.

"Oh no," he said. "Wouldn't want that to happen."

Mort knew better. Tristan craved punishment, because deep down he thought he was a bad boy. Mort was starting to wonder if the answer to the mystery of his lovely mortal was to help him see just what a good boy he truly was.

The chair next to him scraped back. Tristan went to his knees, offering submission for the first time. "I know I don't deserve you," he said. "But I need you."

Mort stared at Tristan, drinking in his beauty. There would never be another moment like this, another first time of submission given willingly and freely.

Tristan looked back, eyes hopeful and lustful. The question *am I a good boy* hung in the air between them, and Mort knew the only satisfactory yes would be his cock buried in Tristan's body.

Mort had no intention of giving it easily. This wasn't about sex to him. He had no real need for sex in the material sense. His desire for intimacy was deeper, transcending the physical. He had already decided this would not be a simple fucking. Tristan liked to have his urges satisfied. But he would have to learn to be something other than satisfied. He would have to learn to wait, to withstand anticipation and uncertainty.

"Please," Tristan whimpered. He was so, so pretty when he begged.

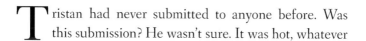

Tristan had never submitted to anyone before. Was this submission? He wasn't sure. It was hot, whatever the fuck it was, and it made it impossible to think of anything else.

He looked up at Mort and craved him. Not just his body, but his approval and his protection. Nobody had ever really protected Tristan before. He had been weathered by existence, the same way the desert rocks got sandblasted in windstorms. It had left him raw, sensitive, and with a perpetual anxiety. But when he knelt before Mort, he felt a comforting blanket made of Mort's mere presence.

Mort stood up, towering over Tristan. He looked down with dark, hooded eyes.

"What is it you want, exactly? Tell me?"

Tristan started small. "I've never seen you without your hoodie off. Can I see you, please?"

"Since you asked so nicely."

Mort's hood fell away to reveal a pale form. His body was muscled, but in a sinewy sort of way. He was not a bulky kind of creature, but he was elegant. And he was marked. Tattoos ran from his neck to his waist, and below besides. They were ancient in origin, but they looked fresh.

"Wow," Tristan breathed. "You look like some kind of a museum piece."

"They're markings of power," Mort explained. "They are the inscriptions and sigils of my father, and the world from which I came."

Tristan reached up with both hands, wanting to touch, but not knowing if he would be allowed. There was something dark and hallowed about Mort's body. He'd barely touched him so far. Mort had sucked his dick, once, but Tristan had laid back for that part.

"Am I allowed?"

"You are. Good boy, for asking for permission."

The praise could have been patronizing, but Tristan drank it in. It was like a warm flow down his spine, warming him all the way to the pit of his belly.

He put his hands on Mort's stomach, ran his fingers over his abdominal plane. He felt the musculature, but he felt more than that too. He suddenly felt a hot pulse of energy that flowed from Mort into his fingers.

"Fuck!" He cursed under his breath and pulled away, looking at his fingertips. They were glowing red.

Mort snatched him by the wrist and pulled him up off his knees, staring at the same parts of him. Tristan tried to pull away, more out of animal habit resisting what felt like a trap, but Mort held him easily, inspecting his fingers with an intense glare. Then he transferred that same glare to Tristan, scaring the absolute hell out of him with a single question.

"What are you?"

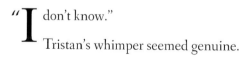

"I don't know."

Tristan's whimper seemed genuine.

Whatever he was, he suddenly reacted with Mort. When his fingers touched Mort's sigils, there was a strong pulse of power, and of recognition. They hadn't hurt each other, but they had scared the shit out of each other.

"Strip," Mort commanded.

"What?" Suddenly Tristan didn't seem so keen to get naked.

"I've never seen you entirely bare before. I need to check you for a mark."

"What kind of mark?"

"Strip," Mort repeated sternly.

"I don't... you are..."

He was scaring Tristan, and he knew it. What he didn't know was why. If the boy was hiding something, Mort had to know.

"The fuck!" Tristan swore as Mort reached for his fly and started pulling his jeans down, underwear as well.

There were plenty of markings on Tristan's body, scars and bruises, and of course bandages from his latest foray into madness. Mort knew he was looking for something special, even as he was forced to tussle with Tristan. He would have liked to have gotten Tris' full consent, but there were some things too urgent to allow him to spend time coaxing a wild thing like Tristan into submission.

"Let me go!"

"Stay. Still." Mort used his reaper voice, the one that calmed even the most alarmed of souls. It should have stilled Tristan immediately, but of course it didn't, because Tristan was different.

Tristan's response to the command was to growl like a feral little animal and contort his body so hard Mort was afraid he was going to get hurt. Not so afraid he let Tristan go, though.

"Fucking asshole," Tristan cursed, losing his manners completely. They would have to discuss this later, his lack of obedience, his refusal to submit to a simple order, and his disrespect. For now, Mort searched his body, pinning Tristan's beautiful, scarred form to the floor. There had to be something here. Maybe not large. Not obvious. But something.

He found it in Tristan's hairline, right at the back of his head where spine met skull. A little silver circle and cross gleaming in his skin. It was pale enough and fine enough that if you did not look with the eyes of a reaper, you might not see it at all.

Mort stood back, holding Tristan by a thick handful of blond hair. Tristan looked up at him balefully, panting hard on his knees with the wasted effort of trying to fight him.

Mort's eyes were so dark they were practically hollow as he intoned, "You've been marked."

"By what? Or who?"

"By a god."

Tristan let out a hysterical laugh. "Yeah. Fucking. Right."

Mort let him go entirely. Tristan scrambled to his feet, naked and mad. He was particularly attractive when he was angry, blue eyes flashing, dirty blond hair tousled from their struggle. Mort wanted to grab him and kiss him, but he thought better of it given Tristan's mood.

"It's true. You are a chosen one."

"Oh, fuck off! What the fuck is a chosen one? Something out of a kid's cartoon? Christ, dude, I know you're death, or whatever, but that's a step too far. Fuck off with that shit."

"A chosen one is someone with powers granted by..."

"Nope!" Tristan interrupted. "No. I don't want to know. I don't care, that's some bullshit. I don't believe in any of this crap."

"Tris," Mort said, making his voice more gentle. "You see demons."

"So?"

"Doesn't the existence of demons at least imply the existence of gods?"

"I've never seen a god once in my entire fucking life. So no. I don't want to hear about this. I don't want to be chosen. I don't want to be weird. I just want to be a normal fucking guy. Where's my beer?"

At that point, Mort did grab Tristan and kiss him, one hand on his cheek, the other hand on the back of his neck, holding him in the lip lock until he felt his angry mortal mate calm and sigh against his tongue.

"Remember, I love you."

"You held me down like a dog," Tristan complained when Mort broke the kiss.

"Yes. I did. Because you were being a naughty pup."

Mort saw warmth and mischief return to Tristan's eyes.

"Was not," he said, nudging Mort. There was another pulse of heat between them as he made contact with Mort's soul-marked stomach.

"That is going to take some getting used to," he said. "Am I going to get a fire shock every time I touch you?"

"I don't know," Mort said, frowning. "I believe it is a function of the sigils, not my flesh."

Tristan reached around behind his head, his finger finding the mark unerringly now that Mort had brought it to his attention.

"How do I get it off?"

"You don't."

"If I got it on, I can get it off." Tristan's logic was impeccably incorrect.

"You didn't get it on. And if it ever comes off, it won't be because you decided to take it off."

If Mort had thought about it for even a second, he would have realized the gauntlet he was throwing down. But he was too distracted by the mark itself, and what it might mean. Chosen ones weren't common in the modern world. Thousands of years ago, you couldn't throw a rock into a crowd without hitting a dozen chosen ones.

The gods were choosier now. More careful. Or perhaps they were lazy and sleeping. Mort didn't pay much attention to them. Once he had determined to quit, he had turned his back on all things immortal. But staying out of the loop wasn't an option anymore. His Tristan belonged to someone. Had been marked by someone. And that would not do.

"Are you angry at me?" Tristan asked the question with a worried expression.

"I'm not angry."

"You seem fucking pissed. And I know, because I'm angry as hell. I don't want a fucking mark on me."

"Don't worry about it," Mort said, while privately worrying about it a great deal.

The mood had been thoroughly killed. They both knew it.

"I'm going to get a beer," Tristan said.

"Good idea."

10

Mort was deep in thought when he heard a whimper from the bathroom in the middle of the night. Mort did not sleep, but he did not hear his boy go in there either. He must have sneaked into the bathroom very quietly for Mort not to notice. Or perhaps Mort had simply phased out of the material world for a time and failed to pay attention.

Either way, that sob brought him back and to his feet immediately. It was a sound of pain, like the kind a wounded animal makes.

"Tris?"

He opened the bathroom door, risking intruding on some very mortal display of bodily functions. Tristan was standing in front of the toothpaste-flecked mirror. He was shirtless, as usual. More unusually, there was blood running down the nape of his neck in a thick flow, then in deltas over his shoulder blades and back.

It was immediately apparent what he had tried to do. He had attempted to cut the mark out of his head. Judging by the tool in his hand, he'd used a fucking screwdriver, sharpened at the tip. As usual, choosing the most simple and brutal solution to any given problem, carving out his own flesh like a sculptor might carve stone.

"Oh, Tristan," Mort murmured. "What have you done?"

"I don't want to be chosen," Tristan said. "Did I get it?"

It was impossible to tell because the area was a bloody mess. Sanguine essence soaked his hair, too, not to mention half of the bathroom.

"Yes," Mort said, telling him what he wanted to hear, lest he continue to try to chip at his head. "You got it."

"Good. I was just trying to clean up, but that stuff hurts like a bitch." Tristan gestured to an open bottle of mouthwash, used as an impromptu sterilization medium. At least he was trying.

"You couldn't have..." Mort dithered for a moment. He had to put more effort into learning how to care for Tristan's physical body. He could not keep stumbling into these situations where Tristan decided that the hammer of self destruction was the appropriate tool for any given problem. "Just, why..."

"I didn't want it," Tristan said. "And you didn't like it on me either. I've never seen you look as angry as you did when you saw that mark. It was like it turned me into a piece of trash. So I decided to dig it out."

Mort looked at the blood smeared over the bathroom counter and Tristan's hands. The room looked like a crime scene. It *was* a crime scene. A crime against self-preservation.

"You did this for me?"

"Yeah," Tristan said, his lips twisting in a wry smile that telegraphed he knew very well how much he'd fucked up, but hoped he wouldn't get in too much trouble. "Do you like it? Maybe now I can touch you without the fiery electric shocks."

Mort took Tristan's bloodied face in his hands and looked deep into Tristan's eyes. He could feel the slight sanguine stickiness beneath his fingertips.

"I want you to understand this," he said. "I want you to write the words I am about to say on your soul. I love you how you are. I do not need you to change anything. Not a single thing. You will never need to carve yourself up for me. Not in any way."

"You didn't like the mark."

"No. I didn't. But I did not want you to butcher yourself. I was unhappy someone had seen fit to lay claim to you while leaving you to suffer to such an extent you considered ending yourself. A mark claims a mortal, but it also implies some responsibilities on the part of the claimer."

"Why didn't you say that?"

"I was trying to recognize the mark, work out where to place blame, and who I needed to go to in order to reclaim you. I am sorry I did not explain myself. I am not used to explaining myself."

"Yeah. I'm not used to... any of this shit. I just want to be normal."

"You're still bleeding," Mort said. "We should bandage you before we speak further."

The bandaging was not good. The place was awkward to get anything to stay on, and Mort was not an experienced caretaker. He tried his best to fasten bandaids and clean cloth over the wound, having cleaned it with soap and water.

"We may need some help here," he said when the blood-wet bandage had fallen off for a third time.

"I don't want to go back to the hospital. I'll just stick a rag on it and hold it there."

"That does not sound like a good idea." Mort prodded Tristan up from the side of the old avocado-toned bath where he had been sitting. "Come on. We need help."

"The wait in the emergency room for something like this is going to be hours, Mort. I'm not going to wait that long. Just leave me be. It's fine."

"It's not fine. I have seen smaller cuts than that become infected and end lives millions of times."

"Oh well," Tristan shrugged.

Mort *snarled*.

Tristan's eyes flew open in fear as Mort's true, dark, dominant nature came roaring forward in a sudden surge that overpowered even this special, stubborn mortal. Mort loomed over Tris, barely containing his anger, and as he spoke it was in the voice of the wind running through the trees beside the river Lethe.

"When this is cleaned and bandaged, you and I will have a very long, very painful conversation about your ongoing inability to value your own life."

Tristan had frozen before him, a little rabbit before a predator larger than it could comprehend. This wasn't the same kind of natural respect other mortals showed Mort. It was a pure fear response.

"Breathe," Mort reminded him.

Tristan let out the breath he had been holding but failed to inhale again.

"Keep breathing," Mort prompted, his voice softening. This boy was so maddening, so perfect, so fragile, and so very *his*.

"Stay there. Do not move. I am going to get..."
"Don't say Tom."

"I am going to get Tom."

"It's two in the morning. And we just woke him up practically yesterday."

"He owes you many favors," Mort said.

"Does he?"

"Yes. A tormentor will always owe a debt to the tormented."

How did he know Tom was Tristan's tormentor?

Tristan's most powerful memory of Tom was back in high school, having his head forced into a toilet bowl and then having the toilet flushed. He didn't share that information with Mort, because he would rather have died than re-live that humiliation verbally.

It was only a matter of minutes before Tom came, shambling with tiredness. It had been ten years since high school, but the sight of him still triggered Tristan. He knew Mort had roped Tom into helping once, but twice seemed a bit much.

"You told me you knew first aid," Mort said.

"Yeah."

Mort pointed a finger at Tristan. "Aid him."

"Christ, Tristan, *again*?!"

Tom's frustration was clear. It was almost like he became the mouthpiece for Mort, who did not make such exclamations with so much energy.

"You can fuck off," Tristan said. He didn't care if he bled out if it meant he didn't have to be humiliated by Tom again.

"I don't want him in my house," he said turning to Mort. "I know you're trying to help, but I'm hard to kill, so you know what? I don't need this. Any of this."

He went to storm out of the front door, but Mort gripped him by the back of the shirt and hauled him back.

"I am not asking, mortal," he said in those ice-cold tones.

"You can't order me around," Tristan snapped back.

Mort's eyes flickered for a moment with deep respect. Tristan was right. Mort couldn't order him around if he didn't want to be ordered.

Mort's tone softened. "Please, Tristan. Let this man be my tool. Let him help you as I wish to help you."

"He is a tool," Tristan agreed. "Fine."

He allowed himself to be sat at the kitchen counter, and he allowed Tom to once again help him. Tom's hands were not like Mort's. They were big and hot and kind of hammy. But they were operated by someone who had taken a first aid course.

To Tom's credit, or perhaps to Tristan's shame, he did not ask why there was a chunk out of the back of Tris' head.

"We're going to have to shave around the area so the sticky stuff has something to stick to," Tom said.

Once that was done, and once a proper dressing with all sticky stuff around the edges had been procured, it was not that hard to fix what had been broken.

"Can I go back to bed now?" Tom yawned.

"Certainly," Mort dismissed Tom.

"Take a beer," Tristan said, feeling especially generous.

Tom didn't take a beer. Tristan was happy about that.

"Very well," Mort said in the voice of an ageless, tireless entity who had still somehow been tired out by Tristan's antics. "I think it is time we both got some rest."

11

"Please don't take matters into your hands like this again," Mort said. "It's not merely that you hurt yourself. It is that you are ineffective when you do."

The next morning had come, and with it, Tristan's anticipation of the long, painful talk about valuing his life.

The talk had begun. The pain had not, but he saw it lingering in Mort's eyes. It was only a matter of time before he was made to hurt in some way. Perhaps Mort would wait for him to heal from his explosion wounds, or maybe he'd be inventive. Tristan felt a sick kind of anticipation at the idea either way.

"I told you last night that you had removed the mark. While that may be physically true, it is not entirely true."

"What's that supposed to mean?"

"The mark was just an indication of the claiming. You can't cut the deeper claim out. It's not on your body. It's on your soul."

Tristan felt a pulse of anger. "You're telling me someone owns my fucking soul."

"That's exactly what I am telling you."

"So if I had..." Tristan made a yanking motion above his head. "I wouldn't have gone where most people would go?"

"You would have been taken into service."

"Wait. Are you saying I sold my fucking soul?"

"That's another way of saying it, yes."

"What did I get for it?" Tristan extended his arms and gestured at his mobile home. "This? All this nothing?"

"It's not uncommon for such bargains to bear little fruit," Mort said. "These deals are often tricks played by lesser gods. I would have liked to have hunted down the deity responsible for marking you, but now the marking is gone, that is going to be more difficult."

"Why didn't you tell me that?"

"I had to think. One of us has to think, you know."

He meant it as a slightly acerbic comment, but it hit Tristan like a jab to the solar plexus.

Tristan felt small and stupid and scared. In Mort's eyes, he was like a toddler who had taken scissors to his hair. Mort might look similarly aged to Tristan, but he had to be fucking old. Like thousands of years old. Compared to his dark majesty, Tristan was a mayfly. A stupid, toddler mayfly.

"Sorry," he said. "I thought I was helping. I'm going to go get dressed."

As usual, whenever he tried to help, things went wrong. He felt the old urge to curl up on himself, to go deep inside and hide every part of himself from the eyes that roamed him.

When he emerged from the bedroom, he was wearing jeans and a shirt, a thick, heavy plaid piece of fabric that functioned more as an emotional shield than as clothing.

"Sorry," he said again, feeling as though he had spent all of his life apologizing for one thing or another. He couldn't get anything right. Why couldn't he get anything right?

Another person might have said something like *it's okay*, or *don't worry about it*. But Mort wasn't a person, strictly, and he did not naturally offer that reassurance.

"We still have the matter of your punishment," Mort said.

"Oh?"

"I promised it would be painful."

Excitement flowered inside Tristan. "Yes," he said. "You did."

Mort put a pen and paper in front of him. "I want you to write down everything you remember about the forty days you spent in the desert."

"That's my punishment?"

"There are few things more painful than memories of bad times," Mort said. "That is one of the reasons souls drink at the Lethe. Forgetting is bliss. But I need you to remember, because that mark was likely given to you there, at a time when you should have perished, and yet survived. Someone saved you. I need to know who. No detail is too small."

"You're a twisted..." Tristan sighed. At least the punishment, such as it was, made some sense, and had some kind of purpose. "Fine."

"Good." Mort turned and made for the door, leaving the kitten in his wake.

"Wait. Where are you going?"

Mort paused, dark shock of hair nearly covering his eyes as he replied.

"I have to see Tom."

Jealousy sparked. Mort sure seemed to run off to Tom every time he got the chance. It wouldn't be the first time Tristan had been looked over in favor of the all-American boy next door.

"Oh."

Mort walked out the door.

Tristan waited exactly thirty seconds before he screwed up the paper and got a beer.

12

"Tom. I have come for the first aid class," Mort announced striding into Tom's garage.

"Oh. That's cool. They're usually run…"

"I would like the first aid class now, please. I do not know when Tristan will next enact some destructive psychodrama, and I need to be prepared."

"Yeah, that dude is wild," Tom agreed. "What's the deal with you two. You hanging out, or…"

"He is mine," Mort said.

"Yours," Tom repeated.

"Mine."

"Uh… so like, usually, you'd have maybe a boyfriend, or like a… husband or…"

Mort fixed Tom with a hollow gaze. "Mine."

"Gotcha," Tom said. "Well, I guess I could drag out the dummy. But I need to get this car ready for Mr Patterson. He said he'd pick it up..."

His reasoning and excuses simply faded under Mort's commanding stare. Tom was so much easier to handle than Tristan, but that was because Tom was common and robust and solid. Tristan was wild, and free, *and cursed*. Oh yes, so terribly, unfortunately, completely cursed.

Tom went into his office and then came out backwards, dragging half a torso encased inside a plastic bag. For a brief moment, Mort was surprised at how interesting Tom had suddenly become, but it was quickly apparent that the limbless torso was plastic. Some kind of oversized doll.

"This is a training dummy," Tom explained under Mort's questioning stare. "It's not weird or anything."

Mort looked down at the plastic form of a person. It was just the first of many strange things in what felt like a bizarre montage of Tom's instruction.

"HA HA HA HA, STAYING ALIVE, STAYING ALIVE. That's the rhythm you have to follow when giving chest compressions," Tom explained at one point, kneeling over the dummy and pulsing at its chest.

It was odd, but Mort was determined to learn everything he needed to take care of his mortal boy.

"Here," Tom said, getting out of the way for Mort to have a go. "You try."

Mort put his hands, one over the other on the dummy where Tom had been working, threw back his head, and shouted the incantation to the sky.

"HAHAHAHAHA STAYING ALIVE."

"No, it's not laughing. It's from the song. Staying Alive," Tom said, clearly perplexed. "And you don't just shout the words, you have to pump the chest at the same time."

"I am not familiar with this composition," Mort replied.

"Compo..." Tom went to his phone and began messing with it, until a pleasing tune of men's voices began to play through the tinny speaker.

"See? It's a song. It has a rhythm. That's what you need to do, follow that rhythm. You pulse and pulse and..." Tom paused again. "Sometimes it feels like you're really not from around here."

"That is because I am not."

"Oh. Cool. Well. No worries, I can teach you. It's just going to take a little longer."

~

I t took a lot longer.

Tristan was not in the house when Mort returned, feeling much more adept and capable when it came to caring for his needs. Tom had given him a plastic bag as a starter first aid kit. It contained several bandages, some medical sticky tape, and compression wrap.

The pen was on the table, being batted at by the kitten. The paper was crumpled up beside it, not so much as a scratch of ink on it.

"You are *such* a naughty boy," Mort purred beneath his breath.

Tristan had not carried out his task. He had shirked his punishment. Tristan wanted to be made to obey. He was never going to just do as he was told. Perhaps that was why the forgotten god had abandoned him.

Mort left the house and walked around to see if he could find any signs of Tristan. He was not an accomplished tracker. In his line of work he usually ended up wherever he needed to be.

It was fairly obvious that Tristan had left in a huff. He could imagine him storming down the stairs off the porch and going... where? He looked around. The goat farm next to Tristan's home didn't seem like it would draw him. Perhaps he'd gone to the...

Mort realized, heavily, that he did not know where Tristan had gone, and that led to a very uncomfortable feeling he had not experienced before. The world, or the part of it that mattered most to him, was out of his control.

He did not like that feeling. He could also do nothing about it. Nothing that did not involve summoning another supernatural and asking them to track Tristan for him, and that would be humiliating.

So he waited.

·   ·   ·

It took several hours for Tristan to return, barely a blink of an eye in the grand scheme of things, but it felt like an eternity to Mort.

He was not used to having to wait. He was especially not used to having to worry. He did both in stoic, static silence while sitting at the kitchen table, the kitten curled up in his hood, occasionally extending a tiny sharp claw into the back of his neck.

Tristan came up the stairs as dusk was falling, like a child coming home for dinner when it got dark. Probably a subconscious routine, something he'd done for years when he was a kid.

Did he come home looking this guilty, sad, and angry then too? From what Mort knew of him, the answer was probably yes.

"Hey," Tristan said as he came in the door.

Mort felt a welling of relief and a surge of irritation. He wanted very much in that moment to grab Tristan and physically punish him, but Tristan was still wounded, and more importantly, Tristan was testing him. How he reacted now would shape their relationship for many eons to come.

So he said something gentle, and something true.

"I was worried about you."

Tristan had known he would be in trouble when he got home, and seeing Mort sitting ever so still at the kitchen table filled him with a nervous energy. Then he spoke. Tristan already felt guilty as all hell, and Mort's mild rebuke, cloaked in care, only made that guilt flare.

"What? You think I can't be alone for a few hours without killing myself? Is that it?"

"If I thought that, you would never be alone."

Tristan scowled. He was in a petulant mood.

"That would get in the way of hanging out with Tom every chance you get," he said. "Don't want to inconvenience you. Are you going to go through every single guy in town, or just the ones on this block?"

"You're cute when you're jealous," Mort observed.

"Fuck you."

Mort sighed.

"But you are also rude, and coarse, and absolutely begging for a beating."

Heat touched Tristan's cheeks.

"I don't know why you came here. I don't know why you're still here. And I don't..."

Mort stood up. Tristan fell silent.

"None of that is true," he said, his voice cool and calm. "I have told you why I am here, because you are mine. Because I intend to claim you and keep you, preserve you against the world. That is why I was not here this afternoon. I requested Tom teach me first aid, so I might be able to patch you up when you inevitably hurt yourself."

Tristan stared at Mort, wrapping his arms around his shirt-less, bandaged body in a gesture of self-defense. Guilt was written all over his handsome face. "You were learning first aid?"

"Yes," Mort intoned. "I was. And you, meanwhile, were supposed to be showing me submission by following orders and taking your punishment."

A slight shrug of a muscular shoulder. "I'm not submissive."

"I know," Mort said. He stepped closer to Tristan, ran fingers beneath the rough stubble of his chin, and tilted it so Tristan's eyes met his. "That is why it will mean so much when you do submit to me."

Tristan let out a breath. "Sorry," he said. "I just... I spend my life trying very hard to not remember anything that happened when I was younger. So you can't just put a pen in my hand and leave me to it. It's not going to work that way."

"Alright," Mort said. "Then why don't you tell me. We will sit, you will talk, and I will listen."

"What. Like you're my shrink or something?"

Mort leaned down and brushed a soft, but commanding kiss over Tristan's lips, feeling the stubble of his mortal's unshaven beard against his eternally smooth skin. "Like I am your immortal master who owns every bit of you, including your trauma, and your pain."

"Fuck," Tristan whimpered under his breath, his eyes lighting up with something like love and relief. "Okay," he said. "I'll tell you."

Nobody usually wanted to listen to Tristan. He'd been jeered into silence his entire life. Tristan knew intellectually that Mort really wanted to know where the marking had come from, but he was prepared to listen to all of Tristan's woes in order to learn that information.

He took a deep breath and started talking.

"I ran away."

"Why?"

"I don't remember."

A lie. He hated lying, but he had to. Mort thought he was broken, but innocent. Tristan could not stand to see the realization in the darkness of Mort's gaze when he realized he was more guilty than anybody else.

"Tom said it was because they sent people to take you away from your mother."

"Oh. Yeah. They sent them all the time," Tristan said. "Maybe that's why. I don't know. I was kind of a handful back then."

"You are kind of a handful now," Mort replied with more than a little fondness in his tone.

Tristan smiled, both at what he took to be a compliment, and also because the lie had now been covered with enough words to allow him to move past it like a shadow in the night.

"Did you plan to... survive?"

Mort was asking if he had tried to off himself in the desert as a ten year old, and the answer to that was no. Tristan had ironically always been a good survivor.

"I didn't plan anything." Now Tristan could be honest, now the lie was dead and buried. "That time I got really lost, I just ran. I ran until I couldn't see anything or anyone and until nothing and nobody could see me."

Mort watched emotions chase over Tristan's face as he recounted the ordeal he'd suffered as a boy, one that had shaped him into the man Mort could not resist.

There were missing parts to the story. He could feel their absence, but he could also tell that Tristan was trying, making a genuine effort to tell him as much as he could stand to tell.

"And when you had run as far as you could?"

"I fell asleep," Tristan said. He was keeping the story very simple, telling it in staccato sentences. But Mort could imagine how it must have been for a boy to run to the wilderness and wake up enveloped in scrubby tundra and rocky hillocks that all looked the same. It must have felt like waking up at the end of the world.

"And when you woke?"

"I was in the desert. I caught some bugs. And I found a stream. There was water to drink and stuff living in it. Toads and some fish and eels."

A small smile flitted over Tristan's face, and Mort built a new picture in his head, one of a boy living wild and free for the first time unburdened by the shame of his mother's profession, or rather, the judgement that accompanied it from his peers.

"You enjoyed yourself."

"I slept under the stars. It was cold, but I didn't care. I had some... extra clothes."

A flash of evasiveness went through his eyes when he said *extra clothes*.

"So you packed before you ran."

"No."

Mort decided not to ask where the extra clothes had come from, sensing he would force Tristan into a lie, and he did not want to do that. He wanted the truth, on Tristan's terms.

"I would have stayed out there way longer than forty days," Tristan said. "I would have lived a lifetime there. I could have survived. I was surviving."

"Why didn't you stay?"

Tristan took a deep breath. "I was worried about my mom. So I came home. And she was so happy to see me, she made me promise I'd never leave again." He turned haunted eyes on Mort. "So I haven't."

Suddenly, it all made sense. That was why Tristan lived in this hopeless town, had not gone to college, or pursued any of the possibilities of the world. He was stuck.

"Your mother has passed. You're not trapped here anymore."

"Aren't I? This is all I know now. And the house is mine. It's not worth shit, but it's mine. I couldn't buy another house anywhere else. I don't have any skills, or education. I scrape by here, because this is where I was made. And this is where I'll stay."

He was describing the impulses of a wounded animal, to den up and to hide.

"So in all that time, you never met any mysterious strangers? Never did any deals with any devils?"

Tristan tightened his lips, and Mort knew what was coming was a lie even before it was spoken.

"No."

Mort sat back in his chair, pensive. He considered whether beating the truth out of Tristan might be an option but discarded that fairly quickly. The boy was still wounded.

There was no immediate rush, he supposed.

And there were other avenues of investigation. Others he could ask about the mark. If Tristan was unwilling, or unable to confess, he would find another way.

"Thank you for telling me," he said. "I know that was not easy."

Tristan colored with guilt. "It's okay," he said, avoiding Mort's gaze.

13

Tristan's wounds healed over the following weeks. With no further demonic visits, he had no reason to create any devastatingly dangerous situations for himself. The two men settled into something like a routine. Mort was largely preoccupied with learning as much as he could not only about Tristan, but the world he intended to live in with Tristan. First aid was only the beginning of his self-education. He bought a computing device and discovered that mortals had created a vast library of videos teaching every aspect of social and practical life possible.

For his part, Tristan seemed to be in a lull of sorts. One could not be wildly chaotic all the time. He still drank daily, but not to excess.

Mort could tell Tristan was restless, not to mention horny. He felt the same way himself. But there were matters to attend to before they could indulge themselves even a little more in physical intimacy.

He had a plan.

A plan that lasted up until Tristan threw a tantrum.

"I can't fucking stand this anymore!" Tristan made the declaration at breakfast time, his eyes flashing bright blue, his chest and abdomen beautifully tight with the rage of unfulfilled desire.

"What is it you cannot stand?" Mort asked the question mildly while knowing the answer. He could smell Tristan's desire. It was contained in bits of tissue underneath the mortal's bed, strewn about and collected inefficiently only occasionally.

This dry spell, as it were, was truly torture for the poor boy. Mort did not mean it as a punishment. He was not withholding for disciplinary reasons, but then again, if he had been, it would have served Tristan right.

"You don't want me anymore, is that it?" Tristan made the accusation with an unintentionally petulant pout.

"Of course I want you." *I intend to kill a god for you,* Mort did not add.

Tristan put his hands boldly to the fly of his pants and started undoing them. He could be very bold and brave when properly motivated. "Then what are we waiting for?"

Mort looked up at the beautiful body of the man he had saved, wondered at the artistry of it. Even through the abuse Tristan had subjected his body to, and the abuse that had been heaped upon him by others, he was exquisite. His hair fell forward over his face, creating a shadow in which his blue eyes gleamed brightly. It would be easy to give Tristan what he wanted. But it would not be what was best for either of them.

Mort reached forward and put his hands on Tristan's thighs. "We have some other business to attend to first, my love."

"Other business?" Tristan looked genuinely confused. He had obviously forgotten Mort's promise, or worse, considered his words to be empty.

"I promised you a reckoning for your reckless disregard for your body, your life, and your position. On your knees, boy."

Tristan's jaw dropped, rough stubble catching the desert light. He did not kneel. Instead, he argued.

"That was so long ago!"

"A matter of weeks is not a long time for a creature like me. I have not forgotten how you spoke to me, your rudeness, your refusal to submit."

Tristan folded his arms over his chest, a defensive posture.

"Do I owe you submission?"

That question caught Mort like a right hook.

On some level, the level on which Mort was immortal and Tristan was a scrappy little mortal, yes, Tristan owed him submission. It was a matter of natural order. But modern people weren't nearly as invested in hierarchy as they had once been, and those who claimed to hold power, or even did have great power were just as likely to be ruthlessly mocked as worshipped.

Mort had not been idle. He had learned much in the past weeks, immersing himself in modern culture. The modern world was a socially flat one, at least in terms of respect. The common folk had disdain for their masters and resented their greed. Mort understood that. He also understood that there was still a craving in some part of the psyche to be mastered, or at least led by a competent leader.

"Owe me submission?" Mort considered the question out loud.

Tristan owed Mort his life, but he did not value that.

"No," Mort finished. "I suppose you don't owe me it. You don't owe me anything."

"Well," Tristan said, half-begrudgingly, half in panic that he might be pushing Mort away. "I owe you something. You've been looking after me for over a month."

"Yes," Mort said. "I have been looking after you, haven't I."

"Yeah," Tristan agreed.

"So perhaps, when I tell you I want you on your knees because you deserve a thorough punishment, you should kneel without asking me if you owe me submission."

Tristan bit his lower lip and emanated a sound halfway between a whine and a growl. He was aroused, because this was the game he wanted to play. The game where Mort made him submit.

One day, Mort would remove these training wheels, and have Tristan do as he was told simply because he was told. But for now he used a firm hand and a guiding voice to put Tristan where they both wanted him to be.

He stood up, fisted Tristan's hair, and dragged him down. His strength was many times that of the mortal, and so it was no effort at all to force Tristan into the submission he craved.

"One day you will be such a good boy you will not need punishment. You will obey with joy and willingness."

T ristan quirked a lip. That didn't sound like him. But he couldn't really argue, because it was clear that Mort was more than ready to *make* him obey.

He was hard as hell. Loving every second of being held this way. Mort had done more than just provide these last weeks. He had made Tristan safe. Tristan had never been safe before, and for that feeling alone he would have gladly given up his self-determination. He was not using his life, or himself. Best that Mort have it all.

The floor was hard beneath Tristan's knees. He looked up at Mort, though not without effort. The reaper's grip was firm. Mort was making sure Tristan stayed where he had been put.

"When I have the claim laid on you removed, I will lay my claim on you in turn. You will be mine, and you will be obedient."

"Or what?"

Both Tristan and Mort's lips twisted at the impertinent question, both enjoying it for different reasons. Tristan loved to challenge, and Mort was fond of being challenged by his boy.

Mort loosed his pants, allowing his great pale cock to spring free. He was long, and he was thick, and he was hard. He had waited more than long enough to do this. Perhaps Tristan couldn't touch his soul markings, but there were none on his cock.

There was only one order left to give.

"Suck. Me."

Tristan's mouth engulfed Mort's cock with an eagerness to obey and please that would have seemed unthinkable if one had only listened to his words.

～

He had done this before. Mort had to wonder with who. Uncommon jealousy threaded through him. He did not like the idea of anybody ever having touched Tristan. Bad enough he be marked. But for someone to have had him this way and left... abandoned him to misery? It seemed unfathomable.

Mort let Tristan suck for several minutes, bobbing his head back and forth, pleasuring and taking pleasure at the same time. The sensations were not new to Mort, but they did have a certain unfamiliarity only because he had not fucked in over a thousand years. When you have forever, sex is less pressing a need.

Tristan was changing that, though. Just as Mort felt himself getting close to release, he reached out, took Tristan by the hair, and stilled him without removing him.

Mort held Tristan on his cock, not so deep that his boy couldn't breathe, but deep enough that he would feel it in his jaw and in the seat of his scarred soul. Questioning blue eyes flashed up at him.

"I am going to keep you here until I think you have learned your lesson," Mort began. "Actually, no, that's not true. You could be here an eternity and never learn. I am going to keep you here until I see fit."

Tristan made some sound against Mort's cock. It was unintelligible, and irrelevant. He didn't try to get up. Mort would have let him go if he saw panic or true intent to escape, but he saw neither of those things and so he held Tristan there for ten, twenty, thirty minutes, until his boy's body began to relax and something akin to submission floated in his eyes.

Tristan was trapped. Caught. Held. And for the first time in his life, none of that made him want to run away. Instead, he felt himself relaxing into the space between Mort's thighs, his jaw aching until he relaxed that too. He felt himself sinking into a kind of calm he might never have felt before.

Was this submission? He'd assumed it would feel bad, or maybe painful. Certainly humiliating. But it didn't feel like any of those things. It felt like Mort wanted him close, and it felt as though he didn't have to make a single decision anymore. Tristan spent so much of his time paralyzed, knowing he was wasting his life, feeling bad about it, but not knowing what to do about it. In this place, that feeling disappeared entirely. He was exactly where he needed to be, doing exactly what he was supposed to do.

Tristan was rock hard, but knew it was not his lust that was to be sated today. This was a punishment of sorts, but more a lesson in patience and delayed gratification. Mort used his mouth as a cock warmer for what seemed like eternity, until, finally satisfied with Tristan's submission, he gave a few languid yet powerful pumps of his hips and filled Tristan's mouth with his seed. Tristan drank it down eagerly, swallowing without being prompted.

"Such a good boy," Mort praised, running his fingers through Tristan's hair. "This is what awaits us when I lay my claim upon you. We will have a lifetime together, and you will always be under my protection, and my care. Doesn't that sound nice?"

Tristan nodded dreamily. He felt buzzed, but better than a beer buzz. This was a Mort buzz, and he wanted to feel this way all the time, even if it meant his balls ached with denial. Even if it meant he had to wait to get what he wanted. He had faith Mort knew what he was doing and was in control, and that was a greater pleasure than any sexual release.

Mort had been putting off discovering the god responsible for Tristan's mark because Tristan clearly needed him to be a stable and constant partner while he healed. The mission to remove the mark would be challenging in many respects, and Tristan would have to come along in order to have the mark removed. With Tristan's display of submission, Mort began to feel his boy might be ready for what lay ahead.

"We are going to travel," he told Tristan, running this thumb lightly over the swollen lower lip of his cock-swollen mouth. "And in our travels it is important that you submit to me just as well as you did today. We are going among creatures like myself. Do you understand?"

Tristan nodded, his eyes still hazy. He was so aroused he had gone past the point of needing to come and slipped into that perfect place of submission that swallowed him up like a drug.

Mort brushed Tristan's hair back from his head. "I need to visit a friend. I will not be gone long, at least, I will try not to be long. Please, stay home and be good for me. I will be back as soon as I can."

14

Mort found Balthazar lounging by one of the more scenic and sandy banks of the Lethe. He was in a great gold tent, attended by many beautiful men and women, but even among the chatter and glitz, he noticed Mort right away. A broad smile passed over his handsome, kind features, and for a brief moment, Mort wished he could bring him good news.

"Mort! I did not expect to see you," Balthazar greeted him. "Have you decided to return to your eternal labors?"

Mort ignored that question. He had no intention of ever returning to work.

"I have a favor to ask," Mort said, crouching down in front of the king. "Do you know what this is?"

Mort drew Tristan's mark from memory in the sand. Balthazar, wise as he was, squinted at it for only a moment before knowing precisely what he was looking at.

"Isn't that Loki's mark? One of his older ones?"

Mort groaned inwardly. He had hoped for it to be the mark of a lesser, more niche, more totally forgotten god. Not one currently enjoying a resurgence, not one who reveled in trickery and who would refuse him what he wanted simply to watch him squirm.

"Why would Loki have claimed Tristan?"

"Why does Loki do anything?" Balthazar shrugged. "He is a law unto himself, and cannot be predicted, nor understood."

That somewhat sounded like a description of Tristan too. Maybe there was a connection after all.

"Any idea where to find him?"

"Everybody is on vacation," Balthazar said, gesturing to his cavorting companions. "The beaches are popular this year."

Loki was not hard to find. Everybody knew who he was, and everybody was keen to leech off a little of his current glamour. The problem with being an ancient god was staying relevant, a feat Loki seemed to manage with little issue because he was happy not to be taken seriously.

"We're going to the beach," Mort informed Tristan upon his return.

"We are? Cool. I think the nearest beach is eight hours away, and then it's not really a beach, it's more like a lake."

"The beach we are going to is not the kind of beach you'd find on a map," Mort clarified. "It's a place outside space."

Tristan grinned. Mort rather wished he wouldn't. This was serious business.

"You will be walking in the realms of gods," he explained. "I need your total obedience. Do you understand?"

"Sure," Tristan said. "Should I bring a towel?"

"No," Mort intoned. "Actually, yes. Never forget your towel."

They drove to the beach together, which was more of a formality than a necessity, but Mort figured it would be easier for Tristan if he at least pretended they were moving through physical space to arrive at their destination. In turn, Tristan obliged Mort by not asking how it was that the patch of desert they ended up at, the same patch he had escaped into as a child, had suddenly become oceanside.

Where rough red hillocks had once stood with rocklike resilience, now bright blue and white waves crashed and dashed themselves against one another before spreading out into pretty foam patterns morphing across ethereal sands. Tristan took this supernatural geographic shift very much in stride, impressing Mort immensely.

Tristan was chaotic, but that meant he had a very high tolerance for chaos, too. Mort found himself falling deeper in love with his boy every passing moment they spent together.

"I've never seen the ocean before," Tris said, blithely ignoring the fact that he wasn't technically seeing it now either. No mortal had seen this place before, as far as Mort was aware. This was not a beach. This was *the* beach, the archetype of all beaches. The sun shone bright in a clear sky decorated with just a few fine wisps of cloud. The air tingled with that saline and iron edge so familiar to many, crisp and refreshing with every breath. The sand was not the organic grit of the desert, but rather it was a fine golden hue.

"Is this where they get the sand that goes through the hour-glass?" Tristan asked, crouching down to scoop a handful, then letting it drift between his fingers in a fine golden haze.

"Yes, actually," Mort said, gesturing around them. "These are the days of our lives."

"Is that a cabana?"

Tris pointed to a shanty-style piece of construction topped with palm fronds. It looked carelessly and casually thrown together, but it, like everything else here, was impeccably perfect.

"Yes," Mort says. "And that is why every good beach has one."

He was scanning the area, looking for... ah. There he was. Mort would have known Loki anywhere, even at a great distance with the god himself little more than a speck.

"I want you to keep your distance," Mort instructed Tristan. "Stay here until I call you over."

"Got it," Tristan said. He was shoeless, and in his usual jeans and nothing else attire. He fit into the beach vibe perfectly. Mort, on the other hand, was a dark, overdressed figure walking out past the populated areas of sand toward a figure who had positioned himself at a distance.

"Loki," Mort greeted the man he found lying on a towel on the sand. Loki was wearing shorts, a garish red and green Hawaiian shirt, and big black sunglasses. He had the form of a middle-aged man with dark hair and wickedly handsome features, rakish, and angular, and incredibly untrustworthy.

Loki lifted a half coconut full of some kind of beverage at Mort.

"Refill, per favor!"

"I have not come to refill your beverage, Loki. I have come to request you take your mark off my mortal lover."

Loki pushed his sunglasses up into his hair and regarded Mort with a darkly amused gaze.

"If you want something from me, perhaps you will do something for me." Loki shook the coconut back and forth. "Refill, please."

Mort had been instantly turned into a servant, but he would do far more than bring drinks in order to claim Tristan.

Mort trudged through the sand back to the eternal cabana where the drink had originated, and ordered another. He took it back to Loki, who took a long sip while providing Mort with no more acknowledgement than a wink.

This was going precisely as Mort had imagined it would. Loki was fucking with him, as Tristan would put it, simply for the sake of fucking with him.

He waited, patiently.

And then he waited a little longer.

And then he started to lose his patience, as well as his temper. The moment he had seen an immortal mark on Tristan, he had been ready to take life. Loki was not taking him seriously. That was a mistake.

He reached into the interior of his hooded sweater and pulled out a scythe, spinning the long handle and making the blade glint and sparkle with sunlight. His impatience made him even blunter than usual.

"Remove your mark. Forsake your claim. Or die."

Loki smiled languidly in that eternally amused way. It had the effect of making Mort yearn to wipe the smile off his smug face.

"You are adorable," he said. "The reaper of human souls, threatening a god as if he had any power or sway at all. You are no god. You are a servant. You are a porter. You are the bellhop in the hotel of the divine. You are nothing."

"He may not be a god. But I am."

Anubis' entrance came with such incredible swagger dust storms threatened to roll across the beach.

Mort had never been happier to see Anubis than he was in that moment. He needed backup, and as much of an ass as Anubis could be, they were cousins in death.

"Two psychopomps," Loki noted. "And one of rank. This is becoming very interesting, isn't it. Fine. Show me the mortal who is worth all this trouble."

Mort retrieved Tristan.

"We are going to speak with the one who marked you. Be respectful. If at all possible, be silent."

"I'm going to meet a god?"

"You are. And a very unstable and dangerous one at that. Follow my lead, and for the love of all that is unholy, don't say anything unless you absolutely must. I am having enough trouble keeping myself contained. I do not know if I can contain the pair of us."

Tristan nodded and squeezed Mort's shoulder. "Don't worry. We've got this."

Mort brought Tristan to Loki, who had not bothered to move from his lounging spot on the sand. He did have his shades up, though, and his mischievous eyes lit up when he saw Tristan. Mort felt a twist of jealousy as recognition dawned on Loki

"Oh, this is the guy? I remember this guy. He was only a little guy last time I saw him. Hey, guy!"

Tristan regarded Loki warily. "Hey," he said.

"You don't remember me, do you? It's okay. I didn't look back then like I do now." Loki looked at Mort. "They never remember. It's kind of cute. They're like amnesiac puppies."

"You remember him?"

"Yes," Loki says. "He's a lucky little guy."

"I would like to lay claim. I will make a commensurate offer for his life, and you can continue your beach vacation."

"Makes sense," Loki said. "Seems simple. Straightforward, even."

Mort knew then and there Loki had no intention of making this simple or straightforward. He was being toyed with, and he was in no mood to play.

"Did he tell you why I marked him?" Loki asked the question when Mort did not speak. "Of course not, he doesn't remember. Not the marking, anyway. I'm sure he remembers the sin."

Tristan shifted uncomfortably next to Mort.

"Whatever sin he has committed, I am sure..."

"Don't be so sure," Loki interrupted with a broad grin. "It was one of the big ones."

"How could it have been? He was but a child."

Loki laughed. "Let me show you why I marked this boy."

Loki snapped his fingers and suddenly, all three of them were in another sandy, dusty location. Mort recognized it as being part of the desert not far from Tristan's home.

"Oh fuck," Tristan groaned. Mort felt his boy press closer to him, as if afraid.

It was night time, but there was a large moon casting more than enough light to see a slow, strange procession working its way across the rocky ground.

A slim boy with a shock of blond hair was pulling something behind him on a wagon. Something much larger than him. Something unwieldy and wrapped in plastic. Mort had seen more than enough bodies in his time to recognize one.

The boy pulled, and he pulled, an expression of pure determination on his face. He was unmistakably Tristan. Those eyes, and moreover that expression, had not changed.

"That," Loki said. "Is a ten-year-old boy looking to bury a body with a plastic shovel." He turned to Tristan. "That's you. You were an adorable little murderer."

Mort turned to Tris, waiting for the explanation, but feeling only guilt emanating from the man he loved.

"He touched my mom," Tris mumbled, avoiding Mort's gaze. "And not like the others. He was hurting her. I knew she wouldn't do anything. So I waited for him to leave, and then I hit him. With a knife."

Mort did not have the heart to correct him and say that technically he had stabbed the man.

Tristan's shoulders slumped with grief. Not grief for the man who clearly deserved it, but grief for himself, for the boy he was, and for the man he had never become. This act had twisted him, rotted him. This act had become the core of his being, the shame and the fear that had driven him to drink and cemented his status as outcast. Mort saw it all clearly in an instant.

"I found this little guy, doing this in the desert," Loki said. "And usually, I'm a hands-off sort of dude. But, sometimes they need help, you know? So I helped."

The boy stopped his wagon and started to dig. He did not have a proper shovel. He had a plastic spade, and by all rights, it should have snapped the second it hit harder rock. But it didn't. It sank into soft sand which began to pour away almost immediately, slowly at first, and then faster, as if a plug had been removed in the bottom of the solid world.

Young Tristan scrambled back as an unexpected sink hole opened up in the desert, sucking down the spade, wagon, and the body before filling itself over.

"That was me," Loki smiled broadly, in case anybody had missed the point.

"I put my mark on him," Loki said. "Because he needed protection. You owe me thanks, not threats."

"Perhaps," Mort acknowledged. "But if you would be so kind, I would like you to relinquish the mark now, so I might take the burden."

Loki cocked his head, his eyes glimmering with mischief. "I am still technically his guardian. And I don't know if you're a suitable match for my little murder boy. It seems like the two of you don't really know each other. The kid didn't tell you about his murder? That's a basic getting-to-know-you sort of thing. I tell all my lovers about my murders."

Mort was unbothered. "It does not matter what he did. I do not judge him. I applaud him."

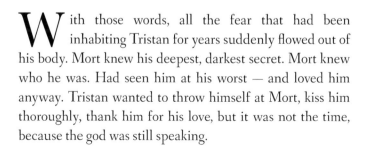

With those words, all the fear that had been inhabiting Tristan for years suddenly flowed out of his body. Mort knew his deepest, darkest secret. Mort knew who he was. Had seen him at his worst — and loved him anyway. Tristan wanted to throw himself at Mort, kiss him thoroughly, thank him for his love, but it was not the time, because the god was still speaking.

Loki had missed this revelation, too intent on his own agenda.

"Prove to me that your love is true, mutual, and moreover, *honest*, and I will remove my mark. You have one year. I love setting arbitrary deadlines."

Tristan looked at Mort, who for the first time, looked less than all-powerful. He looked supernaturally sullen.

"Are there any criteria, specifically?" Tristan started talking, though Mort had forbidden him to do so. It seemed to him that Mort was far too furious to speak right now.

"The reaper will live with you, murder boy. And as for the rest of it, I'll make my decision as to whether or not your love is true the same way the Supreme Court defined pornography. I'll know it when I see it."

"This is why I quit," Mort muttered under his breath. "This kind of god bullshit."

Tristan found Mort so relatable in that moment. Getting pushed around and kicked about by bigger, meaner beings was his life story.

"I love you," Tristan said, wrapping a consoling arm around Mort's shoulders. "And don't worry. I don't have anything else to lie about."

"It's not that simple," Mort growled. "With this god, there will always be another challenge, another stumbling block. He is toying with us because he can. Like a cat with two mice."

The kitten in Mort's hood let out a little *mew* at the word *mice*.

"I will see you boys in one year's time," Loki said, lowering his sunglasses again.

Mort firmly but gently pressed Tristan away from the recumbent god. The murder scene had faded. They were back on the beach. Loki had seen fit to bring matters to a close, it seemed, but Mort was not having it.

He stepped forward, casting a long, grim shadow over Loki's body.

"You forgot something about me," Mort said coldly. "Or perhaps you never knew it, you being a god, me being a lowly psychopomp."

"Oh?" Loki tilted his sunglasses up just a little.

Mort leaned down and smiled the sort of smile nobody ever wants to see. It was a smile that made even Tristan take three big steps backward. Whatever was coming, he did not want to be in the blast radius. He'd learned that lesson thoroughly.

"I have listened to the begging of millions of souls since the beginning of time, and not once have I taken mercy on a single one of them. Do you know why?"

Loki smiled, delighted at this feisty turn of events.

"Do tell."

Mort's voice deepened, resonating with eternity.

"I am the reaper. I do not make deals. **I take lives.**"

The scythe swung. The kitten in Mort's hood jumped and grew. It had not shown any sign of getting bigger in the several weeks Mort and Tristan had been together. It had remained stunted, a little baby cat. But it was a baby no more. And it was a cat no more. Claws extended into silvery scythes, as teeny kitten feet turned to massive, murderous paws.

The beast was leonine and sabertoothed, a feline predator of the collective consciousness, and Mort was astride it.

"Holy shit...."

It was the most terrifying, hottest thing Tristan had ever seen. Mort's hoodie and jeans were now a robe, a robe that hung open from his shoulders, muscular chest and abdomen bared, soul markings glowing with his ire.

Tristan had never seen Mort this way, both deadly and reckless. It was the hottest thing he had ever seen.

"My, my, look at you," Loki purred, admiring. "You are *spectacular* when you are angry."

"Defend yourself, god," Mort snarled, twirling his scythe to the side of his dark mount.

Loki rose to his feet, his Hawaiian shirt fluttering in the breeze. Tristan had the distinct feeling they were no longer on the same beach they had been before, and when he tore his eyes away from Mort, no easy feat, he discovered that they were still at water's edge, but the water looked deeper, greener, and it flowed rather than surged. They were next to a river. An ancient river. They were at Mort's home, or on the porch, at least.

Loki grinned, wild, reckless, and *pleased* at this turn of events.

They were not alone. There was an audience. Charon, the ferry man, and Anubis, the jackal-headed god stood at varying distances, looking on as if to witness the fight.

Tristan saw them and knew who they were in the same way mortals have always been able to recognize psychopomps. He was the only thing out of place here, the only living mortal thing. He was the prize over which these titanic forces did battle.

"Show me what you've got, little reaper," Loki encouraged Mort with an indulgent tone that only encouraged Mort's rage.

Mort urged his black mount forward, making a brazen forward attack. Kitten was massive but agile, big paws covering massive amounts of ground. Mort's scythe seemed as large as the curve of the moon as he swung it toward the smirking god. It truly seemed as though Loki would have nowhere to go.

But Loki was not a fighter. He was a trickster. And that meant his first move was unexpected. Mort had come to kill, but Loki did not have that kind of skin in the game.

He transformed before Mort could hit him, and taking the form of a serpent, he slid into the waters of Lethe, green and gold scales undulating until he surfaced behind Mort and Kitten.

"Missed me," he laughed.

Tristan could already tell this was going to go poorly. He wished he could tell Mort to stop, but there was no talking to Mort now. The reaper was in a rage, and it was that rage that was his downfall.

Mort leaped from Kitten's back and charged at Loki, dark robe fluttering in the wind through the perpetually leafless trees of Lethe. He was so very angry, and so very determined to shed the blood of the god who stood between him and his boy. He was not thinking clearly. He was not thinking at all.

The end of the serpent's tail snaked out from the water, coiled about his ankle, lifted him up and slammed him down on the ground hard enough to make his scythe shatter into a thousand spinning, gleaming shards.

In the distance, Anubis palmed his face.

Loki kept him pinned easily with the serpent's tail as he strode back toward Mort, twin horns curling from his dark, wet hair. He was more handsome now, more angular, more masterful, less amused.

He emitted a tutting sound as he looked down at Mort, shaking his head with what felt like disappointment. For his part, Mort glared up into the gaze of the god.

"You could have made this easy," Loki said. "You could have gone away and been sweet to one another for a year. But you had to test me, little reaper. And now I have to punish you."

Loki crouched down next to Mort and touched him with an affectionate graze of his fingertips. It would have been easier to take if it had been a cruel slap, but Loki knew that.

Mort felt his reaper essence sliding away. He felt the shades of night slip from his skin. He felt himself made mortal. His heart began to beat in his chest. He drew breath. It was awful.

He was hungry. He was tired. He hurt. Not from wounds, but all over, a hundred little aches. He wondered if he was sick, but quickly realized this was just how humans felt.

"I will see you in a year," Loki said with the firm, yet affectionate sternness of a parent who has been forced to punish a son. "Now you must not only demonstrate love and honesty, but humility."

15

Mort woke up in bed. He had never woken up in a bed before, and the tangle of sheets frightened him for a moment until he realized what they were, and that he was not alone. First he felt Kitten curled up next to him. Then he heard Tristan's voice.

"Mornin'," Tristan said affectionately. "You sleep like a log."

Mort had also never slept before. It had been a general lack of experience, which was not so bad compared to all the things he was experiencing. The light coming in through the windows hurt. Looking at Tristan's gorgeous stubble-covered face hurt.

Mort closed his eyes and wished with all his might that he had not made the series of choices he'd made. The memories were flooding back, prompted by Tristan's enthusiastic recounting.

"That, what you did down there. That was so, so cool," Tristan said. "I've never seen anything like it. Kitten turned into a... and you..." He didn't fill in the blanks, there was no need. Mort knew precisely how cool it had been, right up until it had been not cool at all.

"You can say it. I got my ass kicked."

"Sure. But you got your ass kicked for me."

"I didn't save you, Tristan. I didn't get his mark off you."

"I didn't need saving..." Tristan pointed out. "You wanted to claim me."

"And I was the one who ended up claimed." Mort did not need to look to know he was marked. He could feel Loki's touch burning through him, a curse and a humiliation.

"It's okay," Tristan said.

"It's not okay. I have been made mortal! Do you understand what that means? It means I will get sick, get old, suffer, and die."

There was a long pause in which Tristan sat on the end of the bed and looked at Mort as if he were looking at a spoiled little brat. Mort did not enjoy that expression on Tris' face one bit.

"Like me and everyone else?"

Mort took a deep breath, realizing he was unlikely to get sympathy for being mortal from mortals.

"Like you and everyone else," he confirmed.

"It's not so bad," Tristan said, attempting to comfort him.

"When I met you, you were trying to hang yourself."

"Sure, but that was a bad day."

Mort groaned and rolled over. He felt his body, a meaty living thing with meaty living needs. It would not suffer him to rest. It demanded a trip to the bathroom, and it demanded sustenance. How demeaning.

Tristan had been worried about Mort, wondering if he was going to wake up at all. He had woken up himself not that long ago, with Mort in the bed. The god Loki must have put them there, positioning the pair of them like a little girl playing with a doll house.

"Hey, at least we can fuck now."

"Sure." Mort was obviously forcing a smile. "We can fuck now."

"Not right now," Tris said, giving him an out. Mort didn't look aroused. Mort looked miserable and regretful. Tristan couldn't help but feel guilty. This had all happened on his account. "You need some breakfast."

Tristan coaxed Mort out of bed and to the breakfast table.

"It feels like a pancake sort of day," he said.

Mort nodded, staring out the window.

Tristan didn't know what to do with Mort in this state. As far as Tristan could tell, nothing had changed. Mort looked exactly the same, but from context he could tell that Loki had stolen his immortality, or something like that. Maybe Mort would explain later.

"So, you're human now?"

So much for later. The question just fell out of his mouth unprompted.

"Mortal. Yes. The god took my immortality."

"Well," Tristan said. "That sucks."

"Your talent for understatement continues to impress," Mort said, his tone bitter, but not at Tristan.

"It's going to be okay. He said he'd come back in a year. And there has to be a way to get your immortality back. So. Let's just have some breakfast now. One thing at a time."

Tristan made pancakes.

Mort did not eat the pancakes.

S MASH! CRASH!

The tinkling of broken glass emanated from the rear of the house.

Tristan got up to see what was happening and found Mort. He'd been giving him some space to come to terms with things. Mort didn't want to talk. Mort was humiliated, and angry, and afraid. Tristan knew what it felt like to feel all those things, and also knew that sometimes a pair of sympathetic eyes only made it worse.

He found Mort out at the back of the house smashing beer bottles. He had adopted Tristan's mode of dress, throwing his hoodie to the side and standing shirtless and tattooed in the sun.

Tristan didn't intervene at first. He stayed and he watched as Mort hurtled bottle after bottle at the old shell of a pickup truck. His rage was quite beautiful, and entirely impotent.

Once Tristan had finished admiring him, he noticed the way Mort stumbled, and how close he was to hurting himself. A yard full of smashed glass was not a safe place for someone in Mort's state.

"Hey," Tristan intervened. "Why don't you come inside?"

Mort ignored him and hurled another bottle. It caught the rusted protrusion where the wing mirror used to be and exploded into fine glass powder and bigger chunks.

"Hey. Buddy." Tristan started talking to Mort as if he were a frightened dog, not his immortal master. "How are you doing there?"

Tristan caught a strong whiff of beer as Mort reeled around to face him.

He was *drunk*.

"Oh shit," Tristan cursed under his breath. "Look at you."

"I'm mortal," Mort slurred. "I'm MORT-al!" He let out a hyena laugh, threw up, and passed out.

Tristan was left holding the floppy body of the man he loved.

He lifted Mort up, carried him inside, and put him in the avocado-hued bathtub. He was going to have to teach him about self care, like bathing and showering, and teeth brushing, and not drinking a crate of beer in one fucking go.

"**W**arm," Mort intoned as he came around in the water. That was a relief to Tristan, who had worried quite a lot about what would happen if Mort slid down under the water. He'd kept the bath practically empty for that reason. But now, as Mort opened his eyes, Tristan started running the water again.

"Yes. You're in the bath."

"Bath," Mort repeated.

"Mhm," Tristan said. He'd washed most of the filth off Mort so far. There was really just his hair to do, and now that Mort could support himself, Tristan could do that without worrying he'd accidentally drown the man he loved.

Tristan massaged shampoo into Mort's dark locks, scrunching his fingers in Mort's sandy hair. He was such a mess right now, but the sound of pure pleasure Mort made when he felt the scalp massage was one of real enjoyment.

"Feels nice," Mort said, becoming more coherent. "That's the first thing that has felt nice."

"A lot of things can feel nice," Tristan said. "Sex, for instance."

"You still want sex with me? In this pathetic mortal form?"

"Watch it," Tristan nudged the back of his shoulder with a smirk. "I'm in pathetic mortal form too. And you wanted to have sex with me."

Mort tilted his head back, and dark eyes flashed up at Tristan. "I wanted... I *want* to claim you. To own you. To possess you so completely nobody else will ever be able to put a finger on you."

Reaper or not, Mort was still Mort.

"You can still do that," Tristan told him.

"Hmmm..." Mort said, as if he wasn't sure. He was hazy and still very drunk, and Tristan did not want their first time to go that way. Aside from any moral concerns, he could only imagine how furious Mort would later be not to have been in control.

"But first, you need to get cleaned up. And we need to go into Perdition to get you some clothes. You're not going to be able to wear the same hoodie and jeans every day anymore. Mortals get dirty."

"You wear the same jeans every day."

"Maybe I could stand to clean up too," Tristan admitted.

Mort woke in the middle of the night with a painful erection.

Tristan was asleep beside him, snoring happily, one hand wrapped around Mort's bicep possessively.

Something was throbbing in Mort's ears. It took him an unpleasant few minutes to work out that it was his pulse.

Disentangling Tristan as carefully as he could, Mort got up. He had not anticipated mortality being so very challenging every second of every moment of every day. No wonder so many of them never got anything done, and what a massive achievement that any of them had ever done anything at all.

He went outside again, not to drink or to break things, but to look up at the stars, to try to feel part of the world beyond the mortal plane again. Night time was the time the veil was thinnest.

Everything was different as a mortal. He had a headache for the first time in his long history of existence. His mouth felt like sandpaper and tasted like dirt. He'd observed these effects in Tristan long enough to know that he was experiencing a hangover. He didn't like it.

Alcohol had been an escape, but it had solved precisely nothing. He was still in precisely the same situation he had been in earlier, except now he felt worse.

"Hello, cousin."

Mort got a hell of a fright when two obsidian eyes ringed with gold appeared before him. Anubis loomed out of the dark. Before, Mort had always been able to feel him, but his dulled mortal senses did not pick up the presence of the divine.

"I told you not to try to save him," Anubis spoke in the voice of the night. Mort could no longer adopt the voices of places and planes. He was stuck using his very limited voice box.

Clouds skidded away from the moon, revealing the obsidian length of Anubis in all his glory. Mort had to fight the urge to fall to his knees. Mortal instincts were a bitch. So much fight, so much flight, so much *fear*. It was an ever-present undercurrent, infecting every thought and interaction.

"You are just as reckless and self-destructive. You were just stronger. For a time. And now you are weak. As you deserve to be. Do not worry, cousin. When the time is right, I will come for both you and your boy."

The old Mort would have told Anubis to fuck off. The new Mort whimpered.

16

Tristan took Mort shopping the next day. They both got haircuts. Well, Mort got a haircut. Tristan got a trim. He liked his hair long, and Mort agreed. More specifically, Mort told the barber that if he took more than an inch off Tristan's hair, he'd end him.

The second barbershop they went to after being thrown out of the first honored the trim request, this time without the threat.

They both ended up in much the same clothes they'd always worn, except newer versions. Walking through the streets of Perdition, Tristan paused outside a shop called Fancy Guy.

It was the sort of place that hired suits and sold cheap ones, but it made Tristan's eyes light up anyway. Mort saw desire in that gaze.

"What is it?"

"You'd look hot in a suit," Tristan said.

Mort was not interested in changing his attire, but Tristan looked so excited about the prospect of him in a suit, he did not want to disappoint him. He still had money. It was the only power left to him as a mortal. He wanted to use it to make Tristan happy.

Mort did look hot in a suit. Mort looked so fucking hot, it was all Tristan could do not to fall to his knees and start sucking him right there. A crude thought, but with Mort's tall, dancer's body being shown off to perfection, long legs, powerful shoulders and a lithe waist, Tristan could barely contain himself.

"I cannot believe I ever found someone like you," he said. "You're strong, and you're smart, and you'd do anything to have me... and you're so incredible. And everything you sacrificed..."

He knew he was babbling. Tristan had never been that eloquent, but he wanted to let Mort know how much he appreciated him and wanted him and, fuck, it was hard. Literally and figuratively.

Mort's lips quirked as if he were amused.

"We have to go home," Tris said. "And you have to stay in that suit, and I am going to show you just how much yours I am."

The suit had powers of some kind, Mort was sure of it. He could not feel from whence they came, but they turned Tristan from a fairly stoic guy into an effusive, cock hungry man. He could not hide his lust, which was fine by Mort. He found arousal very distracting and satisfying at the same time.

Having somehow managed to survive the drive back from Perdition with an inordinate amount of mutual groping, the pair broke the front door of the house, falling through it, kissing. Mort was shocked at how powerful his lustful urges were now as a mortal. All his hungers were greater, as well as his thirsts — and there was no doubt he hungered, thirsted, and lusted for Tristan.

He pinned his mate face down over the kitchen table and bared Tristan's ass. There was cooking oil on the counter. Mort grabbed it and drizzled it over the generous muscular mounds of Tristan's ass. The oil made him gleam invitingly.

"Fuck, yes," Tristan moaned, guttural and needy as Mort used his fingers to spread his ass and watched as slow rivulets of oil traced their way down the cleft of Tristan's rear, pooling in the dark, inviting hole waiting for Mort.

Mort looked and loved for a long time. Perhaps for too long, because Tristan started to get restless, squirming over the table.

"Stay still," Mort commanded, laying an oil-wet slap to Tristan's ass. "I want to savor this. I want to enjoy you slowly."

"Of course you fucking do," Tristan moaned.

Mort reached around, finding Tristan's cock rock hard. "Don't complain," he said. "You're enjoying this too."

"I just want you to fuck me," Tristan moaned.

He was so impatient. So petulant. So disobedient. Or.. was he? Since Mort had become mortal, Tristan had stepped up. He'd begun to do the things for Mort he should have been doing for himself all along.

Mort leaned over Tristan and let his teeth graze over his ear. "I am absolutely going to fuck you," he promised.

His own cock was throbbing hard too, demanding satisfaction. It wanted to penetrate a tight, deserving hole. It wanted to claim another living body and make that body its vessel. It was so simple, so primal, and Mort was sure it would be so very satisfying.

He took his time exploring. He wanted to draw this moment out, wanted to make it meaningful. But in the end his cock started to physically hurt from desire and every instinct in his mortal frame told him the solution was to drive it deep inside Tristan's tight body.

"Have you been taken this way before?" He asked the question before discarding it just as quickly. "I do not care. There will be no others after me."

Tristan let out a moan, arching his hips. Mort had been rubbing his rear for some time, pressing his fingertips intermittently against the bud which promised to flower around his cock.

His ass was ready, if the way his muscles relaxed every time Mort put pressure there was any indication.

Finally, Mort freed his cock, and fisting it, pressed the head to the gleaming, oil-covered slit of his lover's rear. He took a last few moments as a mortal virgin, sliding his sensitive head up and down before settling into the natural niche of Tristan's ass.

Clamping Tristan's ass between his palms, Mort pressed forward. He felt muscular resistance for a moment, and then he was through, the head of his cock meeting with a welcoming, hot, lubricated embrace.

"Fuck!" They swore the same word at the same time.

"I don't know how I kept my hands off you this long," Mort groaned. "You feel so damn good."

He slid deeper inside Tristan, feeling the hot grip of his mortal lover's body like a vise, and feeling his own pulse quicken, his own flesh suffused with pure pleasure.

It was in that beautiful, fleeting moment that Mort realized Loki had not successfully punished him. Loki had given him a gift. He would never have felt Tris this way before. It would have been an act of mechanical domination and limited pleasure.

This way was meaningful. This way was worth the wait. He slipped more lube around the base of his cock and surged in again, sliding deeper, feeling himself in some real sense become Tristan, or Tristan become him.

The sounds Tris made were incredible, guttural moans and animal growls, sounds of wanting and of need and of connection.

Mort wrapped his arms around Tristan and pinned him down, needing to dominate and to claim. That had not changed, and would never change.

He tried to take his time, as much as was humanly possible, but with every thrust his lust charged more intensely, his balls tightening up against his body. Everything in him wanted to come. And when Tristan began to push back on his cock, offering himself up with beautiful submission, it was more than Mort could bear.

He came hard, shooting loads of mortal semen inside his chosen vessel, and felt Tristan's cock pulse, flex, and follow suit. Semen spread over the kitchen table and leaked out of Tristan's rear as Mort slowly pulled out.

"I've made a mess of you," he said, not at all apologetic.

Tristan uttered a little sob.

Mort pulled him up, immediately concerned. He then became confused when he saw Tristan's eyes shining both with tears and joy.

"What is wrong?"

"Nothing," Tristan sniffed. "I've just been waiting for that for so long. I've needed you, and finally I have you."

"You've got me," Mort affirmed, kissing Tristan deeply. "You'll always have me." He reached around Tristan, gripping his lover's ass and pulling him close. "I don't ever want to make you cry... unless you deserve it," he added as an afterthought.

Tristan snorted gently. "I know you think you've changed so much, but you really haven't changed at all. Mortal or immortal, you're still a bossy..."

"I prefer the term dominant."

"Same same," Tristan laughed.

"It's only the same because a dominant has a submissive, whereas I have a disobedient brat who doesn't see the point of obedience."

"You understand me so well."

"Yes, I do," Mort smiled. "And I will spend the rest of my life ferreting out any little pieces I do not understand and adding them to my comprehension."

17

Sex changed everything. Sex, Mort discovered, was a salvation to mortals as much as it was a means of reproduction if carried out between woman and man. It soothed his soul. It made him calm. And it brought him closer to Tristan. It almost made him feel as though he finally had laid his claim.

"Maybe being mortal won't be so bad after all," Mort said, halfway through a stack of pancakes. Tristan had started cooking more now they both needed to eat, and Mort had no idea about food whatsoever.

Tristan smiled at him. "It has its perks."

"I will have to decide what to do with my life," Mort declared. "Perhaps something medical. I like the idea of saving lives. It feels deliciously ironic."

"I don't know if people want their doctor finding their health issues deliciously ironic," Tristan pointed out. "Looking after people requires empathy."

"I have empathy."

"Sure. For me. But not for most people. You barely notice them."

"Should I? Notice them?" Mort frowned slightly as he poured more syrup on his pancakes.

Tristan leaned across the table to plant a kiss on Mort's syrupy lips. "I love your intense attention, and no, I don't want to share."

Just as Tristan finished expressing his disinterest in sharing, someone knocked at the door. Both Mort and Tristan stared at it. The last time anybody was at the door, it was a demon.

Today, however, it was Tom.

Tristan went to the door, and Mort heard him greet their guest with a taciturn, "What do you want?"

It seemed he was not the only person in their relationship who lacked a certain bedside manner.

Tom ignored Tristan's rudeness and stuck his head in the door anyway, to make eye contact with Mort.

"Hey, guys. There's a bowling league starting up in Perdition, and I was thinking maybe the three of us could get together as a team?"

Tristan and Mort looked at one another. Mort had no opinions one way or another, and so left the matter to Tristan.

"Why?"

"Why not?"

"You haven't asked me to do anything with you in, oh, forever. Now Mort's here, you suddenly want to be bowling buddies?"

Tristan was adorable when he was jealous. He wore it clearly on his face and in the set of his shoulders, the tension of his body. Everything about him screamed *go away* without him needing to say a word.

"I just thought maybe it's time we all let bygones be bygones, you know?"

"I think it would be nice to indulge in some social activities," Mort piped up from the kitchen table. "We were just saying how we have been too insular, Tris."

Tristan glanced over his shoulder briefly at Mort, blue eyes flashing for just a moment.

"Fine."

Tom was excited in spite of Tristan's clear lack of interest. "It's the Bowlerama in Perdition. First playoffs are tonight for the league. I can pick you guys up if you want?"

"We'll drive."

Tristan shut the door in Tom's face.

"Your manners leave quite a lot to be desired," Mort noted, not really concerned, but thinking it worth mentioning anyway.

"He's an asshole. He bullied me for years. Helping you out once or twice doesn't make up for it."

～

The Bowlerama smelled like sweat, beer, and candy. Mort would never have noticed that as reaper. All places were simply backdrops to him then. Now, every bit of it was as real as he was, as mortal as he was. When he stepped into the cavernous space with the balls rolling like boulders and the repeated crash and clash of pins, he became a part of it, and it became a part of him.

Tom was there with three beers, one for him, and one for Mort and Tristan. Tris took his without a word of thanks. Mort accepted his reluctantly. His one foray into alcohol had left him with a revulsion to it.

"Alright, you know how to play?" Tom laughed, as if the question itself were silly. Perhaps it was. The idea generally seemed to hurl a heavy ball down a long lane and try to hit little white pins at the end of it. It was a proto-hunting activity turned into a game, a little window into the many thousands of years of evolution and existence before the modern world.

"You need to swap your shoes out for bowling shoes," Tristan explained as they walked up to the main counter. "Saves the floor, but they're slippery as hell. And don't go over the line or you'll end up on your ass."

Mort wondered if perhaps accepting this invitation had not been a mistake. He did not want to be hurt. He was not used to worrying about that, but the unpleasantness of being hungover was enough warning.

"We can go," Tristan said, catching Mort's look of trepidation.

"No. I want to stay." Mort said. "I want to play."

The words felt odd and inaccurate coming out of his mouth, but he knew he had to begin to integrate into the mortal world.

So they played. Mort was not good at bowling. On his first attempt, the ball skittered almost directly into the gutter.

"Next time, bud!" Tom said cheerfully.

Tristan shot Tom a jealous look. He did not like the attempt at camaraderie. Mort noticed that Tris wasn't drinking as he usually did. Maybe he wanted to stay sharp and aware.

Tris was changing. Evolving. When they first met, Tris would never have come here, and if he did, he'd have been drunk as hell.

"Don't worry," Tom said. "Tonight's a practice night. Everyone's testing their teams. The league doesn't start until next Wednesday at 7pm, so you've got time to get your eye in."

Mort was not worried. Mort did not care about bowling one bit. Now it was Tristan's turn. He stood at the machine where the balls popped out, taking a little time to select his ball.

"You seem to be doing better, dude," Tom said. "You look healthier. More tanned or something."

"Thank you," Mort said, barely listening to Tom. He was far too busy watching Tristan bowl. Unlike Mort, Tristan had a natural talent for physical activity, and watching him was a pleasure, especially the way his pants pulled tight over his ass when he crouched mid-movement to let the ball go.

"Tristan is a handsome guy," Tom said. There was a half-note of jealousy in his voice. He wanted Mort's attention.

But Mort didn't have eyes for anyone other than Tris. Maybe nobody here realized it, but Tristan was special. A mortal like the rest of them, but no normal mortal.

"Yes," Mort agreed, a single word.

Tristan's ball glided smoothly down the center of the lane, heading toward the front pin with almost supernatural accuracy.

"Yeah," Tom said. "His mom was hot too. Pity she was a slut."

Mort's fist was in motion before he could stop it, his hips pivoting, his arm straight. He clocked Tom square in the jaw, dropping him like a proverbial sack of potatoes.

Tristan turned around, celebrating his strike, to see Mort standing over Tom, who was just coming around on the ground. Mort was squared up, legs parted, both fists clenched, looking down at Tom as if daring him to get up.

Tristan gave Mort a questioning look. There were a lot of looks coming their way now, and a furious looking manager with a combover and fabulous mustache making his way over from behind the counter.

"The Perdition Bowlerama is a family venue," the manager said. "I'm going to have to ask you to leave."

"No problem," Tris said, taking Mort by the arm. "We're going."

Mort stepped over Tom's prone body on the way out, as if Tom was less than dirt. That gave Tristan more than a little satisfaction to see. He had not enjoyed what he considered to be Tom's attempts to flirt with Mort.

"What was that about?" He waited until they were in the parking lot to ask. Mort felt tense and angry next to him. His expression was sour.

"He was rude," Mort said. "And disrespectful."

"So you knocked him on his ass in the middle of the Bowlerama," Tristan smiled.

"Yes," Mort said, eyes dark. "And I would do it again."

"You're so sweet," Tristan said, pressing a kiss to his cheek. "I don't think bowling is for us."

"No," Mort agreed. "I don't think it is."

18

Days went by, and then weeks. Time sometimes seemed to pass slowly in the mortal realm if one paid attention to it minute by minute, but paradoxically it also seemed to all flow together and go by very quickly if one stopped noticing.

Tristan and Mort sat on the porch steps together, watching the sun set over the abandoned shopping carts sitting in a tangled heap across the road.

"Do you ever think of moving?" Mort broached the subject. "Now that we have enough money to do that, I mean?"

"I don't know. Maybe?"

Mort noticed Tristan seemed reluctant. He didn't want to say no outright, because he never liked to say no to Mort, but it was clear the answer was no.

"I don't want anything more than this. I don't need anything more than you. You're already more than I could have hoped to have."

"That is sweet," Mort said. He realized something. It had been weeks since the revelation came from Loki, and yet they'd never talked about anything Loki showed him about Tristan.

"We never talked about the murder," Mort said. "I was too caught up in my own self-pity. I am sorry."

Tristan recoiled as if from the memory. "Being mortal will do that to you. And it's okay. I don't really want to talk about it anyway. I want it to be swallowed up by my memories the same way the body was swallowed up by the desert."

"Understandable," Mort said, not pressing the subject.

Then, in a very mortal way, Tris kept talking about the thing he had insisted he didn't want to talk about.

"I killed that man. I stabbed him. And I felt nothing. I didn't feel guilt. I didn't feel fear. I felt like what I had done was right and necessary. It was like having killed a spider."

Mort nodded, understanding.

"I think I'm a psychopath." Tristan gave him a haunted look, voicing a fear he must have been holding inside for many years.

"You're not a psychopath," Mort reassured him. "But you are comfortable with death in a way many are not. Perhaps that is why you see demons. Maybe you allow yourself to see what others will not."

"Maybe. Anyway. I got away with it, like you saw. Not long after that, Mom got sick. And when she got sick, her *friends* didn't want to come around anymore. So it felt like a blessing, at first at least. Until it got worse."

Mort sat solemnly, listening with a deep focus, drinking in every word.

"She was ill for years before she passed. We lived on her savings for a while, then I dropped out of school and did jobs here and there, earning what I could, and stealing to make up for what I couldn't earn. And then she passed, and it was just me. Just this house. I tried for a while, you know. Tried to be normal, to fit in, but I'm not, and I can't. So I gave up." Tristan looked Mort in the eye. "And that's why you found me on the porch. I'd given up on ever being anything to anyone ever again. I felt like the world didn't just not need me. It didn't have a *place* for me."

Mort kissed away the tears that rolled down Tristan's cheeks silently. The pain was still real, even though it was not from the present. Remembering it made it real all over again. It took a few minutes to compose himself, but Tristan stopped crying, and like the sun emerging from rain clouds, smiled instead.

"And then you were just... there. And you changed everything." Tristan gripped Mort's hand. "You are everything to me. And I know they say that's not healthy, you should have self-worth, blah blah blah, but the truth is, healthy people have people. It's how we're made. Being alone, being outcast? That makes us sick."

"You're very wise," Mort said.

"Thank you. And I guess I wasn't alone, after all. I got help that night I killed the guy. I always thought I just got crazy lucky. Can't believe a god was looking out for me."

"Looking out for you. Hm. That is one way to perceive it."

"He saved my life."

"I saved your life," Mort rejoined.

"True, but you haven't hidden any bodies for me yet." Tristan was kidding, but Mort was not. He hated being compared to Loki, especially as the god's seal still lingered on the back of his neck.

"Oh, come on." Tristan nudged Mort when Mort fell sullenly silent. "You're so sensitive."

"Yes. I am. I am sensitive that I tried to get his mark off you, and ended up with it on myself."

Tristan leaned over and pressed a kiss to his cheek. "You might have got your ass kicked, but you looked hot as fuck," Tristan confessed. "You look better getting beaten than most people look winning. Trust me, I know."

"I will always fight for you." Mort turned, gripped Tristan and pulled him close, breathing against Tristan's neck. "No matter how it makes me look."

"That's good. I might need backup, though, given how you fight." Tristan smirked as he spoke, shamelessly giving Mort shit in the way only lovers can.

"I've let you get away with far too much disrespect," Mort laughed, lunging for Tristan.

Tristan squirmed and fought back. Together they tussled, rolling down the front steps and into the dust like a pair of scrappy boys, laughing and cursing at each other until Tristan pinned Mort - and Mort discovered he could not get up.

They realized it in the same instant. **Tristan was stronger.** Tristan saw the realization dawn in Mort's eyes, quickly followed by deep fear.

Tris let Mort go, mostly to relieve the panic Mort was clearly experiencing, not to mention humiliation. There was a small part of him that wanted to press the advantage, show Mort how it felt to be small and to be made submissive. But Tris loved Mort too much for that, and knew how much Mort's dominance meant to him.

Mort got to his feet, breathing hard.

"Well," he said. "That's that then, isn't it."

"That's what, then?"

"I'm not immortal, and I'm not even physically stronger than you. I can no longer provide you with any dominant guidance. I am useless to you."

"Cut it out," Tristan said, sounding more dominant than he intended. "That's not how any of this works. I was never with you because I understood immortality or was impressed with your strength."

"I can no longer hold you against your will."

Mort said that like it was a bad thing.

"Mort, you never held me against my will," Tristan said. "I know that's hard to believe because I seemed like such a fuck up, and you were literally immortal, but trust me, you never did anything I didn't agree to, or at least want."

He reached for Mort's hand and pulled him close.

"You gave up everything you were for me. I'm not going to forget that. I owe you my life. And now I owe you your life, too."

"I want to be dominant," Mort muttered under his breath.

God, he was absolutely adorable when he couldn't be in charge. The sulky, spoiled dom who'd had everything handed to him on a plate of immortality. Tristan loved Mort very much, and because he loved Mort, he had no intention of letting this shit slide.

"You know, I've heard it's good for dominant people to learn what it is like to submit. It makes them better dominants."

Mort eyed him warily with a dark, concerned eyes.

"Maybe..." Tristan said, making Mort's worst fears come true, but with all the love in the world. "... it's time you got on your knees for me."

Mort blushed. And it was adorable, the way the pale skin of his face turned a bright red. The way Mort suddenly avoided his gaze. Tristan suddenly understood the appeal of dominance. It didn't just mean he got to be in charge. It meant he got to look after Mort too.

"I'm not going to do that," Mort said, glancing briefly at Tristan.

They both knew Tristan could make him if he wanted.

"Why not?"

"Because I am in charge of you. I saved you. You are the reckless one who needs guidance, not me!"

Tristan replied calmly. "Which one of us got his ass kicked by a god because he lost his temper and just went apeshit? Maybe the reason we get along so well is because we're not really that different."

M ort had to be in control. Had to be in charge. That was the only way he knew how to function or to feel safe. He realized then and there, covered in dust out the front of Tristan's old house, that being in charge was sometimes just as much about avoiding vulnerability as it was allowing someone else to be vulnerable.

He flickered a glance at Tristan, then looked away again. Was Tris capable of being in control? These last several weeks, he'd stopped his self-destructive ways almost entirely, and Mort knew it was because Tristan had been looking after him.

Maybe Tris had changed. Maybe love had helped to heal some of the wounds on his soul and psyche. Mort couldn't be sure anymore, because Mort was now just a plain old stock standard human with no supernatural insight.

Tris reached out and stroked Mort's cheek, more to get his attention than anything else. When Mort moved his eyes back to Tristan, he saw a new expression in that blue gaze.

"Kneel for me," Tristan crooned, seducing him into submission.

Mort wanted to refuse, or rather, everything in him demanded he refuse. But this was a request the man he loved was making and there were greater parts of him that wanted much more to give Tristan everything he wanted. He truly asked for so little.

So it was that the great and powerful Mort, erstwhile Grim Reaper, sank to his knees before the man he had once entertained ideas of owning.

Tristan looked down at him with a smile, not a smug smirk, but a loving look of pure approval. "You are so fucking hot," he said, his voice thick with love. "And I will do anything for you. I would fucking die for you."

Mort didn't feel like he was submitting. Mort felt like he was being watched over and loved. He felt like he was special, and like the weight of the world no longer rested squarely on his shoulders. In paradox of all his expectations, he felt *free*.

For the first time in his mortal existence, Mort began to cry. Thick tears pooled in his eyes, then ran down his nose and fell to the dry desert sands. He was experiencing true release for the first time, and all from a simple command to kneel.

"Aw." Tristan made a sympathetic sound and crouched down in front of him, shirtless torso rippling. He did not allow Mort to stand, did not release him from the moment of intensity, but he did join him in it.

"You're such a good boy," Tristan crooned. The words went through Mort like a warm wave. "You've always tried so hard, given everything to me. From the moment we met, you've wanted to make me safe and whole. You've loved me so hard, back from the edge. And you've never asked for anything in return. Not once."

"I asked for you," Mort said through his tears.

"And you have me, but you deserve more than that too. You deserve happiness. And you deserve..." Tristan looked up at the home he clung to so fervently. "You deserve more than this old house. You deserve the fucking world."

"I don't need anything beside you."

WELL, DAMN!

The words were not spoken. The were drawn from the creaking of the earth. There was a rumble and a puff of smoke, harbingers of the presence of something very powerful and utterly unpredictable.

"That was quick!" Loki appeared, mai tai in hand, little pink umbrella placed at a jaunty angle next to two brightly-colored orange and yellow straws.

"It would take most gods an eternity to learn humility, life-time after lifetime, but you," he said, propping his shades up on his head, dark sea water wet hair tangling over his shoulders like a cool aunt. "You worked it out in a matter of weeks."

Mort wiped his tears on the back of his sleeve and bit his tongue. He very much wanted to tell Loki to fuck off, but he remembered the consequences of his impertinence from the previous encounter.

"Seriously. Usually a challenge like *love each other and get your head out of your ass* is harder than any of the twelve tasks of Hercules. I'm impressed." Loki drew on his drink, making a bubbling sound with the remnants.

Tristan and Mort looked at one another.

"While you're down there," Loki said to Mort, making Mort think something untenable was about to happen. Instead of any lewd references, Loki plucked something seemingly out of thin air and gave it to Mort.

When Mort turned it over in his hand, he discovered that it was a ring. It was a pretty cool one, made of obsidian, if he had to guess, very sleek, very stylish. There was a small jewel inset into the band, an oval-shaped amethyst. He liked it, but soon discovered it was not meant for him.

"Give it to him," Loki prompted, gesturing at Tristan.

Mort tried to hand the ring to Tristan.

"No! No! No! Not like that!" Loki got down next to Mort, on his knees, so now Tristan had a major deity and his reaper on their knees before him. "Like this...." He glanced over at Mort, to make sure Mort was paying attention. "Tristan, I love you, you're super cool, and so hot. I would get my ass handed to me by the rivers of the water Lethe any day for you. Will you marry me?" He got back up to his feet. "Okay. Now you try."

Tristan and Mort looked at Loki.

"What?"

"Get married. Live happily ever after," Loki said, throwing his arms expansively wide, sloshing mai-tai onto the ground. Where the god's drink landed, little green tendrils immediately began to grow. "I'm a fan of you boys," he said. "My little murder guy and my bratty reaper."

"Do you want to marry me?" Mort asked Tristan the question with curious inflection.

Tristan scratched the back of his head, looking perplexed and excited and a little worried, mostly about Loki. "I mean, yes."

"Not exactly what I'd call poetry, but that counts!" Loki beamed. "I hereby declare you husband and husband."

Mort was not overly familiar with human marital customs, but he did know a proposal and a wedding were not usually the same thing. He also knew that marriage was typically done in the eyes of god, which Loki technically counted as.

"We're married?" Tristan seemed half-happy, half-confused.

"We're married," Mort confirmed. "Forever and ever."

It was Tristan's turn to burst into tears, happy tears of pure joy. Mort got up and hugged him, holding him close. Marriage, he had gathered, meant a great deal to mortals. Tristan had never brought the subject up, but perhaps that was only because he did not dare to do so.

As he was embracing what now seemed to be his husband, Mort realized he was no longer subject to the flaws and pleasures of mortality. His body no longer ached for no reason. His nose no longer ran. He wasn't subject to an irritating high-pitched whine in his ears. He was immortal again. Powerful again. It was a bittersweet revelation.

"Thank you," Tristan said, not just to Mort, but to Loki. "Thank you for everything."

"Yes," Mort agreed. "Thank you, Loki."

"Aw, hell," Loki said, a passing expression of something like shame, but not quite, passing over his features. "I'm going to be honest. Your dad came and told me if I didn't return your immortality, he'd swallow everything I ever loved into the pit of nonentity. So I thought, hey, why not make a whole thing out of it for my two favorite little guys. Alright. I'm out. Do the happily ever after thing, okay? Peace."

With that, Loki was gone.

$\sim$

Tristan clung to Mort, and felt the shift. It was intangible, but very, very powerful. "Are you... immortal again?"

"Yes," Mort said.

"You don't seem happy," Tris said.

For his part, Tristan was happy, and scared, and confused. Everything gods did happened so easily, so quickly, and all at once. He understood why ancient people had worshipped them even while fearing their powerful and capricious natures.

"I liked being mortal with you," Mort confessed. "Not at first. At first it was terrifying, and painful, and kind of gross. But it made us equal. It made us the same. It..."

He didn't finish the sentence, but Tristan had some idea it would be about the submission he had briefly experienced. Mort had melted into that so beautifully once he gave in. It did feel as though Loki's appearance had robbed them both of something precious. Something they both wanted back.

"I'd like to meet your father," he said.

"**N**o. Absolutely not."

When Tristan looked hurt, Mort explained. "My father is not some guy. He doesn't present like Loki. He is the end of all things. He is the void itself. He is formless and eternal, even more than I am. I came into existence. He never did. He was here before anything, and he will be here after everything. Can you understand?"

"Not really, but yes." Tris looked away.

"Tristan." Mort slid two fingers under Tristan's chin. "I love you, and I will spend an eternity with you, and I will give you everything you could ever ask for. But seeing my father would destroy you. A mortal cannot stand in his presence."

"Then make me immortal."

"Sure," Mort said. "I'll go to the immortality store and pick up a box of immortality for you."

Tristan looked hurt by his sarcasm, and Mort immediately regretted it.

"It's not that easy..." he began to explain.

"It seems that easy. I've seen you go from immortal to mortal and back again at the snap of a finger. Maybe we can just ask Loki to make me immortal too."

Mort tried again to explain, but these things were not easy. They did not English well. They were slippery concepts hard to catch in words.

"I'm immortal because I serve a purpose. Loki is immortal because he is worshipped. There would be a price to pay. You would become a servant of something or..."

"Why not you? Why can't I be your immortal servant?"

Mort thought about that for a second. "I mean. I suppose... I guess. Sure. We just have to find some spare immortality."

"You don't have to be sarcastic," Tristan bit.

"Sorry. I wasn't being sarcastic that time. Immortality is limited. And it is guarded, and I do mean heavily guarded. I tried to fight Loki for you, and..." Mort let out a sigh. "I wish I could make you immortal, Tristan. I wish it more than anything in the world. But Loki was right. I am not a god. I am a porter in the underworld, and I do not have that kind of power. I am sorry."

It was humiliating to admit so much weakness, to confront the fact that he could not give Tristan the one thing he had asked for.

"Don't worry," Tristan said sweetly, instantly absolving him. "We'll figure it out."

19

Mort was awake late that night, watching Tristan sleep. No longer could he himself succumb to slumber and drift away into a tangle of limbs and sheets, wrapped up with the man he loved. Instead, he was now a separate thing. He hated it. As much as mortality had been a curse, now immortality felt the same.

He wanted desperately to give Tristan what he had asked for, to reach some place of resolution in their relationship so the happily ever after Loki had so casually tossed out could become reality.

Tristan had asked for immortality, and more than anything, Mort wanted to make that his wedding gift. As the clocks turned one in the morning, it occurred to Mort than there was one store of immortality he had access to, one gift he could give....

～

Tristan woke up feeling better than he ever had before. His head was clear, his body felt light and agile and strong. The ache he'd had in his shoulder for as long as he could remember was gone. Being married was apparently very good for the body.

Mort was lying passed out next to him, snoring softly. Tristan looked down at him with fondness, before the slow creeping horror of realization found him. Mort shouldn't be asleep. Mort shouldn't be able to sleep.

Tristan immediately elbowed his husband awake.

"Mort. Wake up."

Mort's eyes opened, blearily. "What?"

"Something's wrong. You're asleep."

"Am I?"

"Well, not now. But you were. Immortals don't sleep. Sleep is a mortal thing. Something happened. Loki must have come back and taken your immortality. But why would he do that? Why would he no longer fear your father?"

"I don't know," Mort said, snuggling down into the blankets, a cozy, dark shade. Beside him, his kitten kneaded the pillow and purred, looking very satisfied.

Tristan felt the lie. It wasn't merely a suspicion, it was knowledge.

~

"**M**ort," Tristan said, his eyes flashing heavenly blue. "What have you done?"

"Nothing?" Mort tried out another lie. Mortals were always lying. He was sure it was something he could get used to as well.

Tristan gripped Mort by his hair, pulling him up to force Mort to look into his brilliant blue eyes. When he spoke, his words dripped with cool authority. "Don't ever lie to me again."

Mort got instantly hard. That was not the desired response, he was sure, but he couldn't help it. Tristan was fucking hot as an immortal. His skin was clear, his hair was lustrous, and his eyes shone with blue fire. Mort wanted to fuck him so badly.

"Tell me what you did," Tristan insisted, releasing the grip as if realizing it was causing more distraction than good.

"I gave you my immortality. Now you will live forever. I gave you what you wanted. What you asked for."

"I wanted us both to be immortal, Mort!"

"I can't do that. But I could do this."

Tristan looked down at him with celestially beautiful eyes. "Mort..." He said Mort's name with soft regret.

"It's done," Mort said. "And it cannot be undone, not by me. Maybe by a very powerful god, but I don't intend to bring this to their attention, and I'd prefer you didn't reject my wedding gift."

"Your wedding gift is me getting to watch you get old and die."

Mort paused for a moment. "This feels like when I complained about suffering when I was first made mortal, and you having absolutely no sympathy for me whatsoever."

Tristan growled under his breath. "You're a brat as a mortal."

Mort shrugged and smirked. "You're hot as an immortal."

There was a long pause as Mort felt himself inspected by a new immortal gaze. Tristan really was quite a stunning thing. Mort had never wanted to submit before, but Tristan had lured him into it while mortal, and now seemed inclined to continue in that vein.

His instincts were proved correct when Tristan next spoke.

"I'm going to punish you for this, Mort."

"Are you?" Mort could not hide his delight, or his antic-ipation.

"Yes," Tristan said, stern as hell, and beautiful in his newfound power. "I am."

"Do it then," Mort challenged him.

With a curse, Tristan grabbed him and tossed him over onto his stomach. Mort's hard cock rubbed against rucked up sheets as Tristan bared his ass and laid a hard slap across both cheeks. It was Mort's first spanking, and it stung.

"You've been planning this all along, haven't you. You found me trying to end my life, and you gave me all the life. Twisted little devil."

"Not a devil, a psychopomp," Mort corrected, earning himself a flurry of very hard slaps.

"Nothing more than my mortal slave now," Tristan growled. He had settled into his position very quickly and naturally, taking to immortality far more easily than Mort had adjusted to mortality.

"I've wanted to do this many times," Tristan confessed as he spanked. "You've always needed taking down a peg or two, just a little too arrogant, a little too spoiled, a little too reckless."

Every accurate insight was accompanied by ever intensified sting. Tristan spanked hard. He was not nearly as careful with Mort as a mortal as Mort had been with him. He was genuinely pissed at having been put in such a position, and he was demonstrating his displeasure very firmly.

"How dare you," he growled. "Without asking me, without even considering my consent. You were so offended and hurt when Loki did that to you, but you did it to me without a second thought."

Mort thought briefly about apologizing, but he didn't. He didn't because that might make this stop, and he didn't want it to stop. He relished the pain rushing through his body. It was starting to feel like pleasure. His cock ground against the bed with every slap. Tristan's grip and dominance thrilled him and made the pain worth it.

After a lengthy thrashing, his ass bright red, swollen, and sore, he felt Tristan rise up over him, felt his cheeks being spread and knew that his thrashed ass was about to be fucked.

Tristan grabbed the lube from the side of the bed; the same lube they had previously been used for his ass fucking was now going to be used on Mort. Mort heard the top open and felt cool lubricating gel dropping against his ass.

Tristan was silent, grim, even, as he rubbed the lube up and into Mort's hole, pushing his finger in with casual ownership. Mort laid still and submissive, anticipating what was going to happen next.

He felt the bed move as Tristan straddled him from behind, his massive muscular thighs spread on either side of Mort's hips. Big hands spread his cheeks and held them wide. The thick head of Tristan's rampant cock pressed against Mort's tight, un-fucked ass.

"You wanted to claim me," Tristan said, sliding inside Mort's once virginal ass in a stern stroke. "Now I claim you. You wanted the mark removed from me…"

He fucked Mort with powerful strokes, grinding him into the bed, punishing his ass inside and out. Mort gasped and grunted, feeling himself violated and disciplined in the most perfect way.

"But now I put my mark on you."

Tristan bit Mort, his teeth sinking into Mort's shoulder hard enough to draw blood.

"Fuck!" Mort screamed.

It was only the beginning.

Tristan bit and fucked, and punished, absolutely ravaging Mort until Mort felt so completely human, utterly mortal and entirely debased. When Tristan finally relinquished his place, Mort was leaking cum from his aching ass, his cock sore from more than one orgasm forcefully milked from Tristan's rutting. The bed was covered in his semen and his sweat.

He was weak, beautifully, perfectly, pathetically weak. He could hardly focus his eyes, let alone move his limbs. He had been drained, all that nervous human energy transformed to pleasure, pain, and submission.

As he recovered, he looked over at Tristan. Tristan wasn't out of breath, because he did not have to breathe. He was not covered in sweat, because he did not have to sweat. Sitting propped against the wall, one arm resting on a raised knee, his face peaceful and powerful, Tristan was finally all he could be, and he was magnificent.

Tristan caught his eye, replying to the helpless little plea Mort made without words.

"You should have thought about the consequences before you forced me into immortality," Tristan said. "I don't feel sorry for you, Mort. I know you did what you did because you wanted this. Needed it. You've spent an eternity on top, and now it's time you felt what it's like to be the bottom."

Tears gleamed in Mort's eyes, for he knew what had gone unspoken so long had been understood. He didn't have to ask Tristan for what he needed. He was going to get it.

"I am going to take care of you, my marked, mortal mate," Tristan promised. "I am going to love you into eternity."

This was Tristan's gift to Mort. Even in this satisfied state, he saw the hunger in his husband's eyes, and knew without a shadow of a doubt that Mort had never allowed himself to take this role, though some hidden part of him had craved it. Not just submissive. Something deeper than that. Something less and more. Surrendered.

"Go back to sleep," Tristan cooed gently. "I will make pancakes in the morning."

Mort's dark lashes fluttered against his cheeks. He obeyed.

It was still night when Tristan stepped out beneath the stars, sucking in not air, but power.

"Interloper."

The German Shepherd he had once seen in the hospital was standing before him. He saw it for what it was now, not a dog, but a god.

Having already met Loki, Tristan was not impressed. Anubis was great, powerful, and very dangerous — but not to Tris. Tris saw the cracks of age and the bitterness of comparison in Anubis' visage. His presence here was predatory, like his prototype, the jackal. This god had been circling Mort for a long time. Waiting for him to fall. Waiting for him to fail.

Anubis narrowed his jackal-eyes at Tristan.

"My father will not permit this."

Tristan snorted, his upper lip curling. "Your father has no say in this. Loki may fear his power, but I fear nothing. Besides, your father will soon know what I know, what everyone will soon know."

"And what is that?"

"Mort belongs to me."

Anubis snorted.

"You are a jacked up little mortal playing with death, and there is only one way for that to end."

Tristan extended his hand, reaching for something he felt, but could not see. Obligingly, a scythe appeared in his hand, the grip materializing from his fist, lower part of the staff extending toward the ground, upper part reaching for a starlit blade, which curled long above his head.

There was a prickling sensation as little claws made their way up his back. A little white kitten with bright blue eyes settled into his hood and began to purr.

Mort had not just passed on immortality. He had passed on the duty of the reaper as well. Tristan was ready to take on both burdens.

"I am the reaper now, Anubis. I am not like Mort. I understand death. And I know what drew him to me the day he found me trying to kill myself."

"What was that?"

"His own death. A yearning for his own end. Freedom to forget. To be, and to become again. I will give him a lifetime of love, and when it is time, I will lead him to Lethe. I will watch him as he is reborn. And when he is of age, if he chooses me again, I will love him again. He deserves an eternity of happiness, and I will give it to him. Again. And again. And again."

Schwip!

Something pink zipped past Tristan's ear as a slice of ham was flung off the porch, flying past Tristan's shoulder and over Anubis' head.

"Fetch, boy," Mort said from the safety of the wooden deck, safely behind Tristan. "Fetch, fuck off, and don't come back."

Anubis bristled. "You dare disrespect me because you hide behind your mate."

"Damn straight," Mort rejoined without a hint of shame. "Our rivalry is at an end, cousin. You have no business with me anymore. Find another family member to feel superior to."

"You should leave us," Tristan said. "We are not in need of any third wheels."

Anubis made a sound of discontent, a predator deprived of his prey, but under the twin gazes of Tristan and Mort, he took his leave, sinking into the darkness with a certain awkwardness that satisfied Tristan very much. Only when he was sure Anubis was gone, did he turn to Mort.

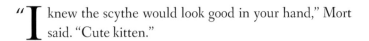

"I knew the scythe would look good in your hand," Mort said. "Cute kitten."

Tristan turned toward Mort, and Mort saw the full force of what he had sensed the very first time he laid eyes on Tristan. This was his rightful, proper, fated replacement. Mort's father would have no qualms with this development, because Tristan was perfect.

He stood like a cold angel under the silver moon, his his ice blue eyes absolutely radiant with beauty, kitten padding in his long blond hair.

"How much did you hear of what I said to Anubis?"

"Most of it."

"Was I right? Did you come here looking for your end? Did you plan this all along?"

"I'd like to say yes," Mort said. "But I am incapable of planning anything. I knew when I saw you that you were special. As I grew to know you, I understood you had a destiny. But I, like you, am a creature of impulse and instinct. Blame destiny. Not me."

Tristan smiled at that. "That's true. Blaming you for the outcome of your actions would imply you had considered them."

"Indeed," Mort smiled, leaning against the porch railing. His black kitten, now becoming a cat, padded over to sit next to him. "Congratulations on your employment."

Tristan leaned against his scythe, already comfortable with the dark tool. "What will you do while I am harvesting souls?"

"I've been watching a lot of television lately, mostly renovation shows. If you don't mind, I'd like to try fixing up this house."

"You can do whatever you want," Tristan said. "You'd do it anyway, probably."

Mort grinned broadly.

"You know me so well."

For the first time in his existence, Mort was not only seen, but known. He was understood. He was loved. Mortality was a small price to pay for such a happy ending.

Tristan twirled his scythe.

"I think I'm going to like this," he said. "Maybe I'll pay Tom a visit."

"You can only reap a soul when it is that soul's time. There are rules and regulations."

"Which I give zero fucks about," Tristan reminded him.

Mort let out a groan, tempered with a smile. "We're all in trouble, aren't we?"

"Absofuckinglutely."